CURSED PRINCESS CLUB
LambCat
I0823019

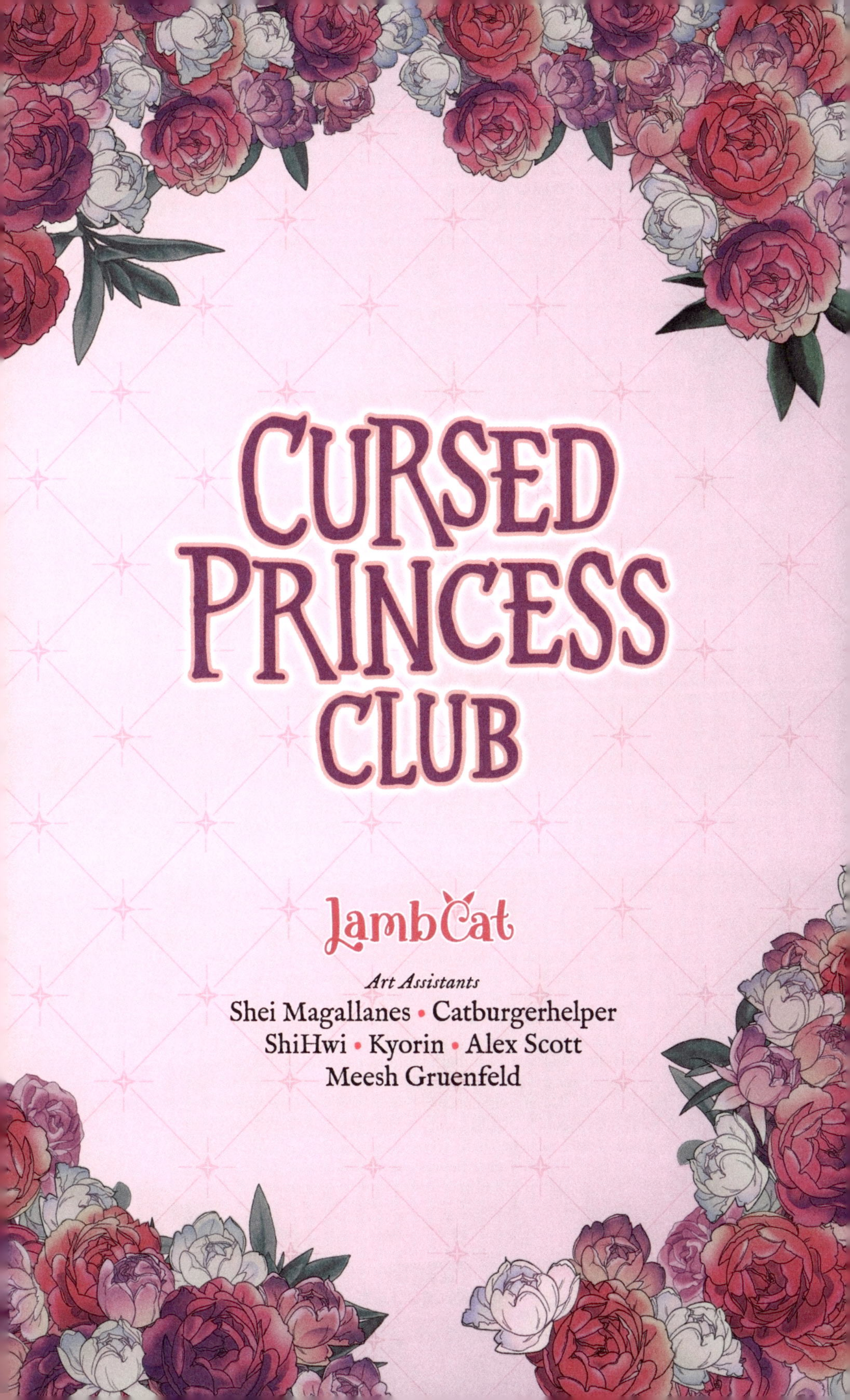

CURSED PRINCESS CLUB

LambCat

Art Assistants

Shei Magallanes • Catburgerhelper
ShiHwi • Kyorin • Alex Scott
Meesh Gruenfeld

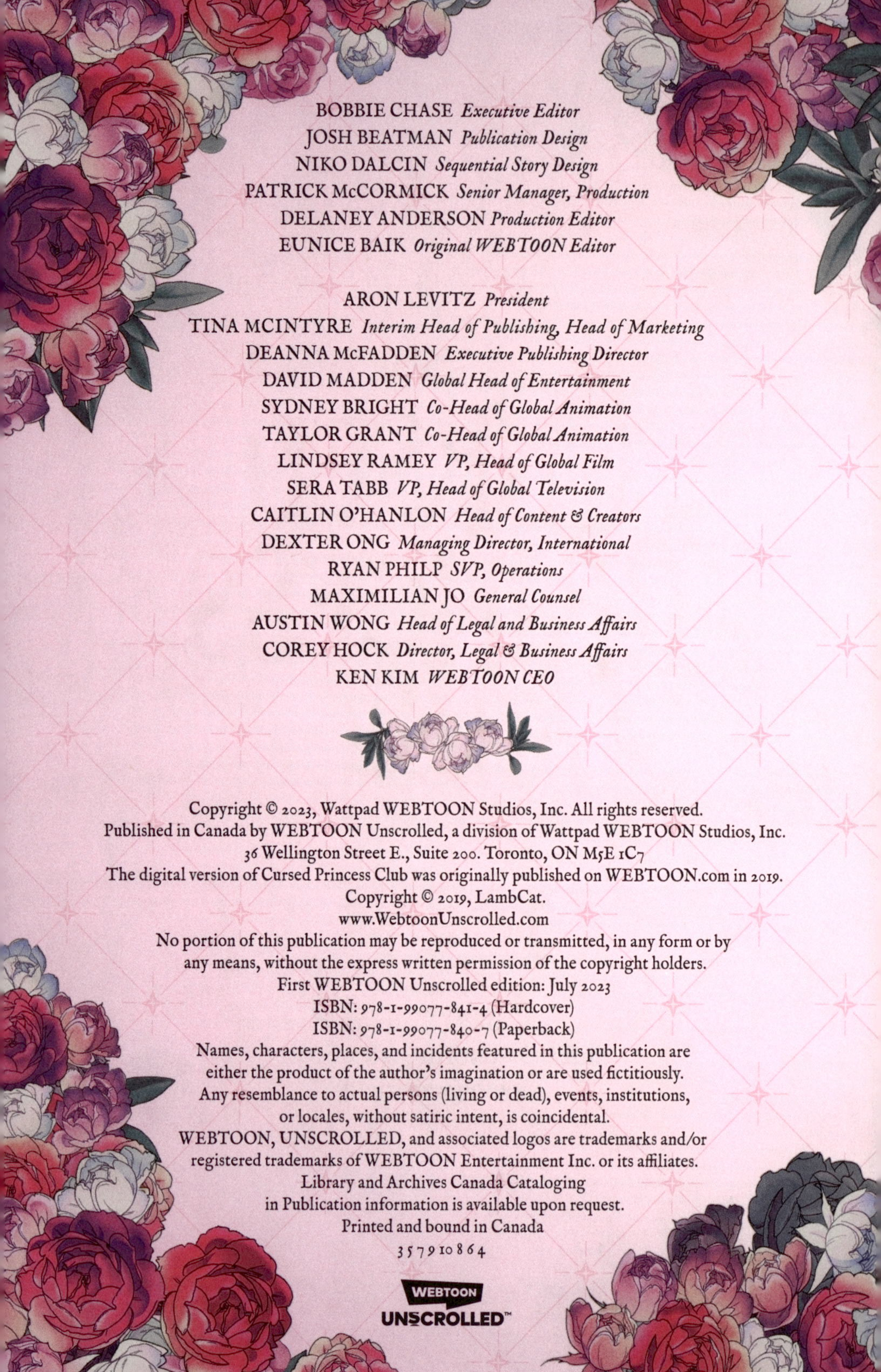

Published in Canada by WEBTOON Unscrolled, a division of Wattpad WEBTOON Studios, Inc.
36 Wellington Street E., Suite 200. Toronto, ON M5E 1C7
The digital version of Cursed Princess Club was originally published on WEBTOON.com in 2019.

www.WebtoonUnscrolled.com

First WEBTOON Unscrolled edition: July 2023
ISBN: 978-1-99077-841-4 (Hardcover)
ISBN: 978-1-99077-840-7 (Paperback)

Library and Archives Canada Cataloging in Publication information is available upon request.
Printed and bound in Canada
3 5 7 9 10 8 6 4

WEBTOON
UNSCROLLED™

Contents

Previously on

CURSED PRINCESS CLUB...

Hubba-hubba...

Princess Gwendolyn and her older sisters Maria and Lorena are betrothed to three hotties from the Plaid Kingdom, and happiness ensues for all couples!

...That is, until Gwen overhears her betrothed, Prince Frederick, declare that he doesn't want to marry her.

Gwendolyn is...is... REALLY UGLY!!!

...Spiraling into despair and self-loathing, Gwen runs into the nearby haunted forest, where she stumbles upon the Cursed Princess Club. She is initiated into the club but not before promising to abide by a few commandments.

"Don't go anywhere near the barn."

LET'S BE FRIENDS, FREDERICK.

FROM NOW ON, I'LL BE WATCHING YOU FROM THE SHADOWS.

Following the group's advice, Gwen successfully communicates to Frederick what she heard him say and that they should just be friends—or so she thinks, because Frederick, unfortunately, did not see it that way.

The Pastel King is gone on one of his many expeditions, which means his daughters are unallowed to leave the palace or let anyone in. Only Gwen is allowed out for her "extracurricular" classes with the CPC (which her family believes is a school for elite princesses).

Gwen seems to be having a strange new problem with her reflection, though...

Chapter 1

Ahh, what a refreshing breeze.
Hmm... By all accounts, I should feel completely relaxed right now.
Ever since I resolved things with Frederick and my family about the engagement...
I thought all the heaviness inside of me would disappear.
And I mean, look! We're all having such a fun time today!
...But I can't shake this feeling that there's something I've been ignoring for a while...

SMASH

REALLY UGLY.

AAAAHHH!!!
Wh-what happened??!!
My face! I can't see anything!!
I...
I CAN'T SEE ANYTHING!!!
—Wait...
pat
pat
...Oh.
sigh
It was just a dream...
But it looked just like what I've been seeing in the mirror.
...I think I need to do something about my face.

That afternoon...
Thank goodness for baking. It never fails to make me feel relaxed.
step
step
Same with the Cursed Princess Club. It's always great to be back.

Good afternoon, Miss Gwendolyn.
Gwen!! Did you bring homemade scones??!

Um, yes! With some fresh honey butter. I hope you like them!

step
step
Pardon my haste, but those look... **immaculate**.
May I try a scone as well?
Oh! Yes of course, Curtis!

chomp

Miss Gwendolyn!! I cannot carry on with my duties as a butler without knowing how you made this!
What can I give you in exchange for the recipe??!
I-I can just write it down for you...!
Hey, Curtis, you can try this honey butter anytime you wa—

SMOOSH
—OW!!
Syrah, can you stop saying vile things to Curtis and hogging Gwendolyn all the time?
There are other princesses here who've been wanting to meet her too, you know!!
Our baby's so popular...

Hi! I'm Princess Aurelia of the Gilded Kingdom.
I only visit the club on some days, but I've been looking forward to meeting you!!
It's really nice to meet you too, Aurelia!

My lovingly overprotective stepfather cursed me with a mouth that will disintegrate any material it touches.

So there will be no true love's kiss for me...

Papa can be overprotective, but he would never do that...
Um, sorry— I didn't mean to dampen the mood!
Would you like to meet my best friend in the club too?
That's her over there!
Princess Renée of the Velvet Kingdom.

Wow, she reminds me of Maria! She's adored by swans!!

?
MmMMmM!!

Oh my goodness, there's a curse that sews someone's mouth shut?!

Oh! No, no, this is the only remedy our doctors came up with for my curse. When I—

—Oh no, here they come...
blegh
whee~!
...
Yep, she and Maria are very similar...
A banshee overheard Renée and her sister gossiping about her...
so she cursed them both to have objects pour out of their mouths whenever they speak.
But instead of frogs, Renée's sister has gold coins spill out of her mouth.
So while Renée has been hidden by her family, her sister gets invited to every party.
Go figure...
You know, I actually think I've heard about this curse.
My sister Lorena loves collecting fairy tales that are... intense...
Oh, but you haven't even seen the intense part yet.
...What do you mean?

See those swans? They don't just surround her because she's beautiful and elegant...
ptoo~

Yep...always great to be back...

All right, everyone, gather 'round and take a seat!

Well, I hope we can talk more later, Gwen!
I'm looking forward to it!
I'm gonna go find a table for these scones.

I hope you're all as excited as I am, because...

...IT'S LECTURE DAY!!!
Ugh, somebody save us...
groan~

Hmm, I feel like a lecture might be kind of nice to take my mind off that dream I had this morning...

step
step
Hi, Jolie, can I sit next to—

—Oh! Your eyes, they look different today!

gasp
Thank you for noticing! Sometimes I carry around different eye masks so I can change up my look when I feel like it.

Ooh, what other masks do you have?
Hmm, let's see...

Okay, everyone! It's time to start a new lecture topic, as we finally finished our last series...
"Financially-Savvy Princesses and the Fairy Godmother that is Compound Interest."

Good, because if she talked about compound interest one more time, I was gonna kick her right in her lectern.
Doesn't even matter that she just personally threw me a prom...

So for our new topic, I thought we'd take a request from our newest member, Gwen!
Kiddo, is there any topic that you've been curious about or anything that's been on your mind?

...Huh?
Me?!
Yay,
Gwen!

Something
that's been on
my mind...?

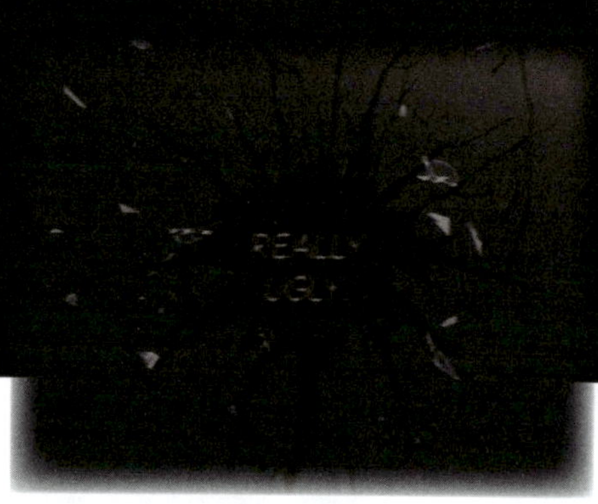

...!!
Um...
Well, I...
...I-I want
to learn...

...h-how to be
beautiful.

Prez!! With all due respect, I cannot allow you to go any further!

A lecture is **NOT** how you teach someone to be beautiful!

Yeah! No more lectures!!

SLAM!

The best way to make someone beautiful is obviously through...

...A **MAKEOVER!!!**

Yesss! We love a good makeover!

clap

MmM mMm!

Well, I think the best way to teach someone how to be beautiful is through meditation!
When your mind is empty of clutter, you can begin to see the natural harmony within yourself!

Yeah...no offense, Jolie, but your mind is definitely **not** empty.
When I had to fish that ping-pong ball out, there was some weird stuff in there...

hahaha

To Gwen
...A note? To me? How long has this been here...?

open
To: Nell

If you want to be beautiful, I can show you a secret.

...Show me a secret...?
Who sent this? And why didn't they write their name?

Wow, Saffron was right. It **is** cluttered in here.
I don't think it was either of them.
What about the other side...?

Glare~
—Aah!

That's Nell. ...Right?

She glared at me before... at the slumber party too...

...Did she give me this note?

Okay, it's settled, then! We'll each hold our own lessons on how to become beautiful!!
Yaay!!!

No!! That is **NOT** how it's settled!!
This is MY club. I have the floor, and you're going to listen to **MY** lecture!!
SLAM!

Okay...
Sorry...
Fine...

Ahem...
Thank you.

Now, let's begin by discussing the earliest documented beauty ritual...
which was to take a hefty mixture of goat fat and mulberries and smear it onto one's face for a fertile glow.
Psst Jolie, can we see those eye masks again?
Sure!

And it's common knowledge that the kingdom whose main exports are mulberries and mulberry-related products is—
ZZZ
ZzZz
ZZZ
snore~
OH COME ON, GUYS!!!!

Everyone drew straws, and Jolie won the chance to lead the first lesson.

Hooray!!!

The next morning at the local hospital...

Like Princess Panda says, "A charitable princess is a sexy princess!"

And I guarantee that after you read to children today, you'll be glowing!

I don't really care what you want me to do as long as I get to wear this cute little outfit.

That's okay! There should be a uniform left out for you in the changing room. We'll meet you up ahead!
Okay, got it. Thanks, Jolie!

There it is.
...In front of another mirror.
shut

I've been telling myself that I just need to avoid all mirrors until I learn from everyone's lessons how to be beautiful...
rustle
...and I can fix whatever seems to be happening to me...

...but I need to hurry because it seems to be getting worse.

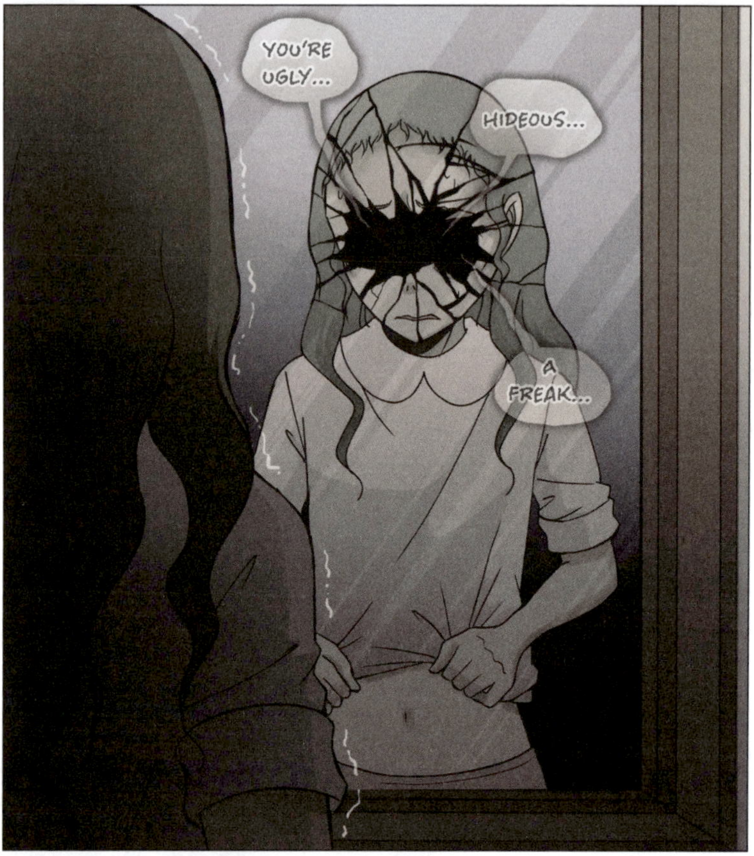

YOU'RE UGLY...
HIDEOUS...
A FREAK...

COME CLOSER...
What it's saying about me...hurts... So why can't I look away?
FIX YOURSELF...
I think I need to let someone see this...

Hey, kiddo, how's it going in there?
knock knock
...Gwen?

I'm coming in, okay?
CREAK...

What is
she doing?

Hey there, kiddo!
Sorry to rush you, but
Jolie's running a tight
ship today.
I was told to
catch you up
to speed on
where you'll be
stationed.
pat
Prez!!
I—

By the way, this
volunteer outfit
looks really cute
on you!
H-huh...?!

—Um, I mean,
you look nice too!
I've never seen you
in a dress!
Aw thanks, kiddo!
I used to wear a lot
of dresses back in
the day, actually...

How is she not
saying anything about
what's happening
to my face in the
mirror?!
Or is this
something only
I can see...?!

I'm glad that Jolie is having us volunteer outside of our little forest.
step step
It's a great way to get out and meet new people and have new experiences.
And it can also impart us with a lot of great life lessons.
For someone young like Abbi, this is a great chance to learn how to be a role model for children. 
You don't **need** to be rescued by Prince Charming, guys! I'm throwing this book in the garbage!!
Why?!! That's our favorite story!!
Because I'm gonna tell you an even **better** story... 
about being rescued by a very tall, cool lady in a pantsuit...!
Ohhh!!

Volunteering is also a good place to learn how to deal with uncomfortable or unexpected situations life throws at you.
step
step
step

Go ahead, Monika.
You can do it!
H-hi, children... We're gonna read a classic fairy tale called um...er... "Th-th-the Frincess and the Pog"...

..."Frincess"?!
I-it's okay!!! You just have to power through!!

Uhh...Look at me, kids! I'm the world's greatest magician!!!
poof!
AAAAH!!!!!

See??
grow~!
clap
clap
Wowww!!

step
step
So you'll be stationed in this wing on the left, Gwen.
Okay!

—Oh! I have to stop you right there, Miss.
Witches aren't allowed down this wing.

They'll gladly help you through this door to the right, though.
What?! B-but wait! I'm not a witch—!

push
HEY!! That's my **witch** right there!!
—!!!

What's been up witch you?
Get it? Cause we're both witches—

SHUT
That was a misunderstanding. I am not a witch. I'm a human girl. This is just the way I look.

Um, yeah, Doc. She's a volunteer. Hence the uniform...
Oh my goodness, please forgive my mistake!

step
step
Um, sorry about that, kiddo.

The mirror is right. I really look hideous...
What are the kids going to say?! Won't I terrify them with my face?

I'm just going to ruin everything. I should leave...!!!
Okay, kiddo! Here's your volunteer station!

GWEN'S HERE!!! OH, I'M SOOO HAPPY!!!
Ugh, thank goodness! We really need you here!!

...You do?

We're holding a puppet show for our kids soon, and we requested you to help us with your many creative talents!
Can you help me fix my puppet?
I keep sewing my puppet's mouth shut on accident.
Um, yeah! I can help with those things!

I'm in charge of making the stage, and I really need help with my penmanship.
PuppetShow
Oh, sure! I think that's pretty good though, considering you have a cursed hand!
...That's not my writing hand...

Hey, kiddo. Your presence around others is more valuable than I think you know.
Jolie brought us here today to show us how to be beautiful, right?

Well, I think it was to remind us that beauty isn't just found in the way we look.
It can also be found in the small, unique efforts we take each day to help one another.

No, no, Gwen said to keep sewing along this line here...
mMmm!

pat
Hmm, I need to bring over more sewing supplies. Do these uniforms have any pockets?
pat

...?
There's a piece of paper in here...

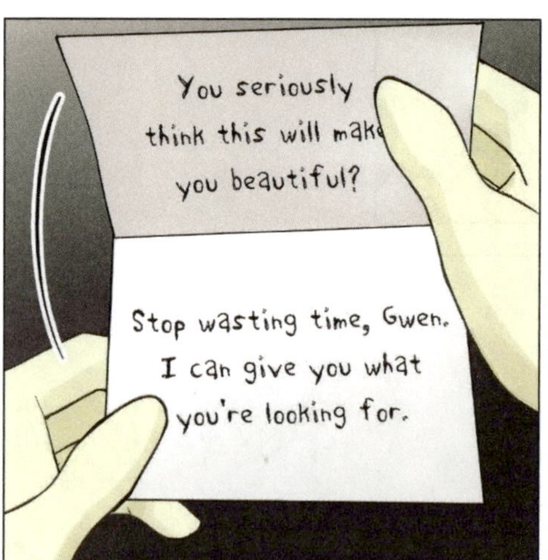
You seriously think this will make you beautiful?
Stop wasting time, Gwen. I can give you what you're looking for.

Where do these notes keep coming from...?!
And do they have something to do with what I see in the mirror...?

Ready, boys?

Let Operation Clandestine Balcony Serenade begin!!

Why do I have déjà vu...?

Chapter 2

Sigh
This is such a stupid idea. Why did I even agree to tag along?

So... why did you, then?
It's not like Dad made you this time.

...Well, because I have something I need to give Gwendolyn...
Bet you do...

It's a **BOOK**, Lance!!!
And, Blaine, can we go home now?!
There's no way we're gonna be able to do anything with those guards on duty!!
Just watch and learn, Frederick.
Well not with **that** attitude...

And the maestro says, "Euphonium? But I barely know 'em!!"
I don't get how that's a joke...
step
step

—Whoa!! Aren't you one of the princes from the Plaid Kingdom?!
Y-you're not supposed to visit here while the king is away!!!

Oh! No, no, I've been touring potential venues in your kingdom to host a gala that I'm on the committee for.
But while I was downtown, I'm fairly positive I saw the Pastel Princesses at Little Miss Muffet's Buffet.
So I thought it was only right to stop by and alert you fine gentlemen about this...**potential oversight**.

What??!! The king's gonna **KILL** us if he finds out they snuck past us and into town!!!
What do we do?!!
We need to get them back here, **fast**!!

It's okay, we can outrun them! Those all-you-can-eat curds'll really slow 'em down!
dash
Nice, Bro.

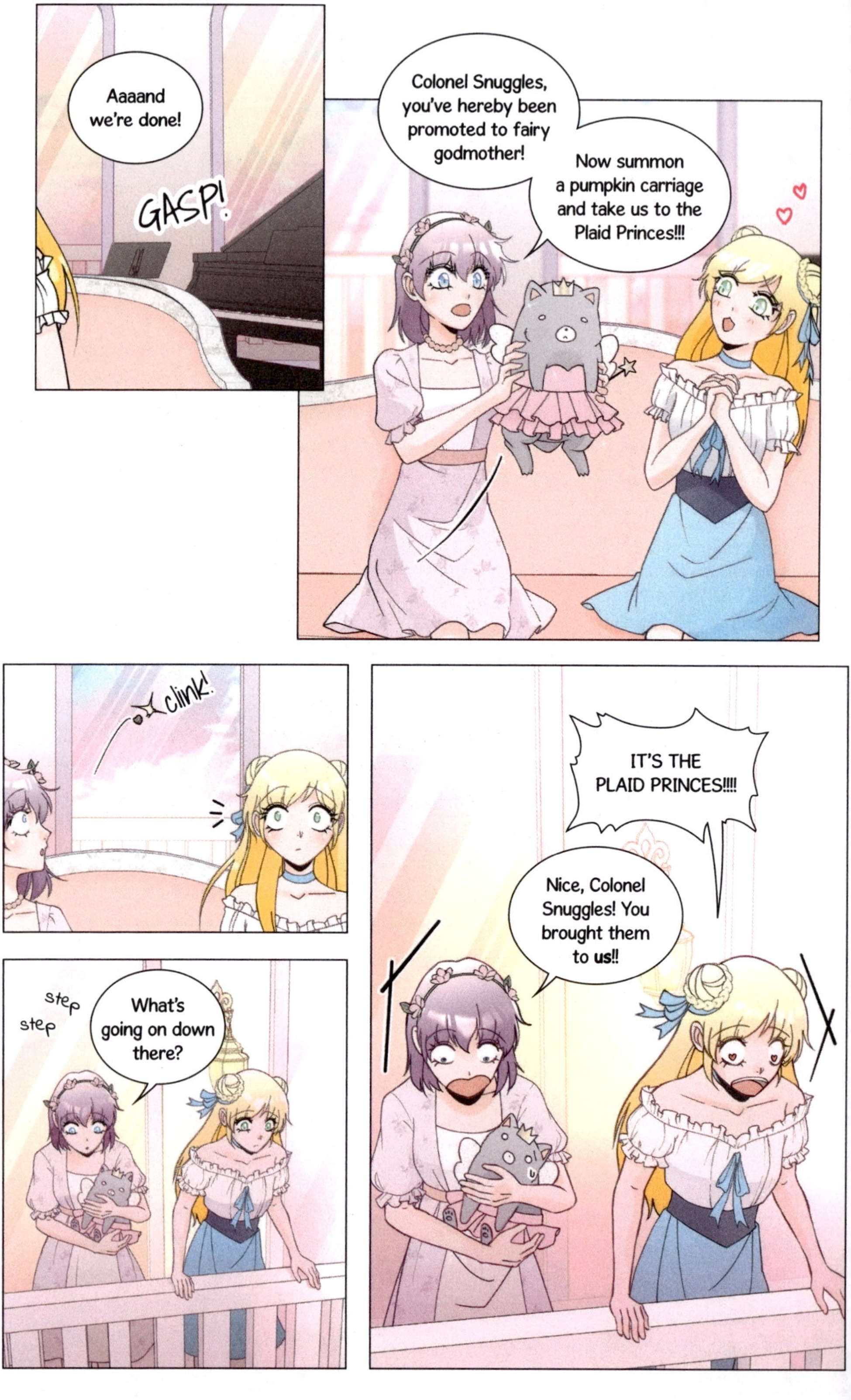

Aaaand we're done!

GASP!

Colonel Snuggles, you've hereby been promoted to fairy godmother!

Now summon a pumpkin carriage and take us to the Plaid Princes!!!

O, resplendent princesses! We apologize for intruding on your evening like this!
But we could not last another day without seeing your beautiful faces!!

We respect your father's wishes to not enter the palace.
But there's no decree against serenading you ladies from outside of it!!

Oh my!! A romantic serenade?! I can't believe this is happening!!
Darn, I really wish Gwen was here for this!!!

Um...is Gwendolyn not home?

She gets an exception to leave home when she attends her fancy-pants elite princess school.
But she'll be really happy to know you visited, Frederick!

Oh... okay.

All right, let's begin, shall we? You guys come in on the four, nice and legato.
And Frederick, your harmonies tend to run minor. We're singing a love ballad, not a requiem, okay?
?
Just start the song...

Inhale~

I **knew** something was fishy.

It's a good thing that halfway down the hill, I remembered Little Miss Muffet's Buffet is **CLOSED** on Tuesdays!!
Tch...

I don't care if you're royalty—you guys are in HUGE trouble!!

Whew, volunteering today was hard work but a lot of fun!
step
step

I'm sure if we discuss this calmly, we can come to a mutual understanding!
There's nothing to discuss! You need to exit the premises now!
—Oh!!

Well, yes...I did lie to trick you gentlemen into leaving your posts. But we meant no harm or disrespect!!
Is something happening outside our palace?

Is everything okay down there??
We don't want to cause any trouble!!
H-huh?! N-n-no, Princess Maria, you did nothing wrong!! You're **perfect**! I-I mean—

What's your name, Guard?

Oh...!! No one ever asks for my name!
I'm Lieutenant Beckett Dandridge, proud footguard of the Pastel Kingdom.

Lieutenant **Dandruff**, was it...?
That's a very childish comeback for someone of your position...
But it still hurt my feelings...

Maybe you simply need to get used to seeing us around here...
...because we're engaged to the princesses, and we're not going anywhere.

Yeah?! Well you're right that you're not going anywhere...
because it's my duty to imprison all of you as **TRESPASSERS** until the king returns!!
Oh, **please** try...

Things are getting kind of heated between them...

!!
step
step
Ugh, what a waste of time...

Someone better come get me when those two stop bickering and it's time to leave.

Why am I hiding from him?

#@!%*
giggle
I'm impressed that he can read at a time like this.

If you're not going to comply, then I have no choice but to use force!!
As if I would ever strike an actual prince!

Don't make me laugh.
WHACK
Whoosh
OH NO! FREDERICK!!!

Huh...?

WHACK!

AAGH!!!

I HATE THIS STUPID, HILLY KINGDOM!!
TOSS

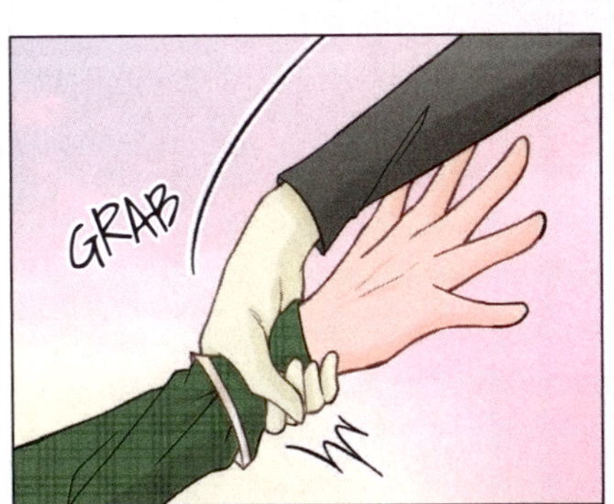
GRAB

Oh my gosh, thank you—

AAAHHH!
YANK

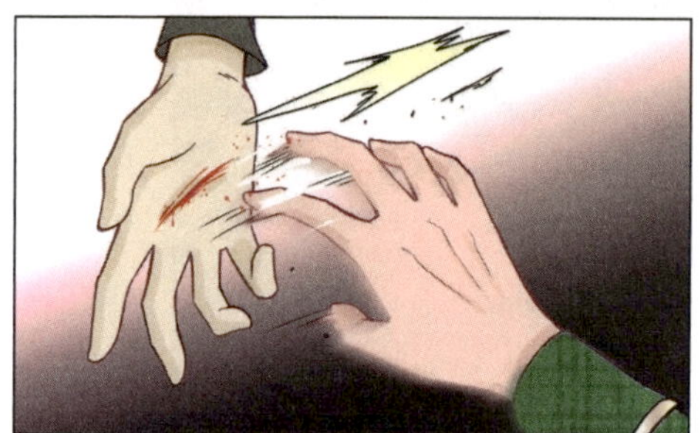

AGH!

WHOOOA—!!

CATCH

Wait,
Gw-Gwendolyn?!!
Was it you—?

GASP
—Oh my
God!!

Your hand's
bleeding!!
Gwendolyn,
let go!!
No, it's okay!
But...I can't lift
you up any
further...
You'll have to
pull yourself up
from here...

pant
gasp

Gwendolyn....

She's hurt
because of
me...

Gwendolyn,
your hand...!
I'm so sorry,
I-I didn't—

I-it's okay.
I understand.
You were probably
frightened by
me...

...I didn't
know she could
make that
face...

Seeing her like that makes me...
...want to...

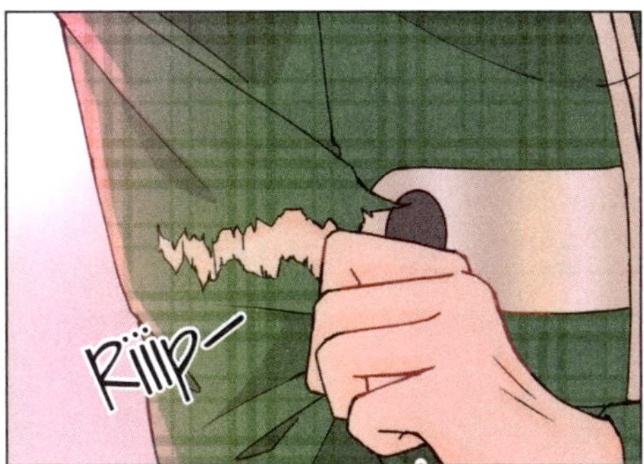
Riiip-

This'll have to do until you make it to your infirmary.
...!!

...

Um, also...

I brought this because you asked me in your letter what my favorite books were.
A-and I thought instead of telling you, it'd be easier to just bring one to you.

You mean I can borrow this?
...If you want...

I do want to!! Thank you, Frederick!

Meanwhile, a few feet away...
squeeze
LET ME GO!! I'm not gonna give in and let you do your stupid serenade!!

Y-you can do whatever you want—I don't care! Just don't hurt me...
...I feel like you're not very good at your job.

Oh, this isn't about the serenade anymore.
This is about you ogling Princess Maria—otherwise known as **my fiancé**!!!
...!!

Well, you're right. I **do** have feelings for Princess Maria.
But I can promise you that I've never **ogled** her before...
...because her looks aren't what matter to me—UNLIKE YOU!

Excuse me?! You don't even know me!!

Oh, I know guys like you!
You only like her because she's beautiful on the outside—but I find her beautiful for who she is on the **inside**!!

Hey, I think Maria's beautiful on the inside too!!

...Do you mean her personality?
...I meant her vomit...

Well, if I were you, I'd stop all this gallant peacocking and start trying to appreciate her on a deeper level!

Or else, once all your shallow tricks wear off, she'll leave you for someone who does!

Lance, go pick up Frederick. I think it's time for us to leave.
I'm on it!
gasp
Mate, are you okay...?

Your Highnesses!!
Yes, Blaine? What's going on down there?!!

Though our serenade was planned with the best of intentions, it ultimately fell flat.
We must depart now and conceive of more resilient methods to express our devotion.

Also, my birthday party's happening soon at our palace.
We hope your dad returns by then and your whole family can make the trip over!
Put me down, Lance!!
step
step

catch
We'll do our best to make it!

Li'l bro, I know it can be tough, but you gotta keep your clothes on at these things, okay?
WHAT. IS. **WRONG** WITH YOU?!!

Chapter 3

Back at the C.P.C...

Finally, the blessed day has come for everyone to flourish under my **superb** leadership!

For today, I shall bestow upon you an activity that is always guaranteed to make you feel more beautiful...

...spending time with plants!

Clap

Clap

Oooh!!

Pretty
impressive,
right??

Uh-huh!
They look, um,
really virile...
W-we like
you just the
way you are,
Saffron...
I WASN'T
ASKING FOR YOUR
COMPASSION!!!

I had no idea
there was a part
of the forest with
a pond like this!
Oh yeah, there's
still a lot around
here that we haven't
shown you yet!

All of these
flowers are tough
on my allergies
though.
I should have
brought some
eye drops...
sniff~
...?

Okay, everyone,
grab a vase! We're
going to do some
flower arranging!

Remember, all flower arrangements are lovely in their own way!
step
step

There we go.
I've been wanting to give you a break from that forced smile you've been holding lately.

Forced smile...

Uh yeah, we all know you pretty well by now, Gwen. Even a blockhead like me can tell that something's up.
It's not good to bottle things up, you know. That's why I like to complain about things **right away**.

So why don't you stop being a polite little princess for a second...
and just tell us what's wrong so we can help already.

Um... Y-yeah.
I **have** been bottling something up...

...!!

I just...I don't even know how to begin to describe it. And it keeps changing...

HIDEOUS...
LOOK CLOSER...

It's happening again...
I...I can't look away...

Um... Gwen? You're mumbling. I can't hear y—
blub
blub

WHOA!!

WHAT THE HECK ARE YOU **DOING,** GWEN??!!

Gasp *Cough*

Um...I-I think something's really wrong with me.
I think I really **AM** cursed, or I'm a witch or something!

Why do you think that, Gwen?

Because I can't see my reflection anymore. I haven't seen my face in so many days...
I just see a shattered face and...darkness...

When did this start happening?!

Um...the night after I talked to Frederick about our engagement.
I remember feeling very relieved because the talk had been weighing on my mind.
And that's when I saw it in the mirror for the first time.

My reflection...It tells me that I'm ugly. And that I need to fix myself and become beautiful.
I feel like I'm pulled toward it and I can't look away...
...because it's right. I **am**—

Gwen.

It's okay. You're not cursed. And you're not a witch.

I think this is something else entirely. Something very **human**.
And though it's curable, it can certainly feel just like a curse.

But I'm sorry you've been going through this alone, kiddo.

So... what is it, then?

Gwen, before I explain, I think it would help to **show** you first.
Would you be up for taking a little trip with me?
Um, okay...

Listen, everyone. I've been allowing you to lead your own lessons on how to be beautiful.
But I'm taking back the reins now.

Psst! Prez, it's really not the time for one of your boring lectures right now—

No. This is a different type of lesson, just for Gwen. I'm taking her to meet some... **acquaintances.**

And I could use your help, Syrah. You too, Saffron.
Sure thing.
Of course. Where are we going, though?

Princels
[*prin.selz*] | An organization of princes who have ostracized themselves from society due to their physical appearance and their inability to find a romantic partner.

A few hours later...

Clop
Clop
Your Highness, we have arrived at your requested destination.

Thank you, Curtis. We won't be too long.
step
step

Would you like me to accompany everyone inside for some extra precaution?
Nah, these guys are the least of my worries in this kingdom, given our history here.
I'd rather have you stay outside and alert me if any prying eyes come around.

Who are these people Prez is taking us to visit...?

knock
knock

CREAK...
Whatever it is, we don't want it.

Is that any way to talk to someone who once saved your life?
GRAB

...
Fine. Come in.

tick
tock

tick
tock

...O-okay! That was a fine attempt at small talk. Let's just get down to business, then.
Everyone, I'd like you to meet...

...the Princels!

They're princes who have shunned society much like us.
But instead of curses, it's due to their insecurities over their physical appearance and their inability to find romantic partners.

Hey!! They're not just **insecurities**—they're serious **defects**, you know.
Don't you see these freakishly giant ears?! I can't go out in public like this! I'm basically cursed!!

Right...
Well, we came here to gain some insight into something you told me once before.
You said that you see something **odd** when you look in the mirror, right?

His ears look fine to me though...

Yeah. A few years ago, I looked in the mirror and saw actual elephant ears growing out of my head.
No one else says they can see it, but I know they're all lying.
To this day, they still taunt and flap at me every time I look at my reflection.

That kind of sounds like what's been happening to me...!
Um, I just see a potato with glasses.
I see literal trash.
Eventually we felt so ashamed and rejected by everyone that we vowed to hide ourselves away here forever.

I'm really sorry that you see yourselves that way.
We at the Cursed Princess Club can relate to feeling rejected by society for failing to meet their standards of perfection for princesses—

Oh will you **shut up** about that?!
No one here has any sympathy for your bogus pity party.
Not when you princesses have it **so much** easier.

Excuse me?!
Any princess, no matter how cursed or marred they are, could bag a hundred guys wanting to marry them.

Well...I guess I never considered things from that perspective...

—Wait. I'm sorry...Did you just say a "**Blaine**"?

Oh yeah. We have our own vocabulary.

"Blaines" are the nickname we give for the best-looking one percent of men who get all the girls...

while all of us Princels get nothing but a lonely and miserable life because of our unlucky genes.

Why does he have a poster of my sister's fiancé...?!
Whoa, that's your sister's fiancé?

...Can I come over sometime?
...

Okay, and honestly, Princels? I don't think you guys look bad at all. I would totally date, like, each of you!
And I'm cursed with a nose that grows when I lie, so you know I'm telling the truth.

Well, I don't want a chick who'd date just **any** loser!!!
Your nose totally looks huge right now. You ARE lying!!
You're not my type, so I wouldn't date you anyway!!!

...Huh?!

Hey! Be nice to my friend, okay?
Don't point at me with your giant ham hands!!

HAM hands?!!!
Um, I brought some pie...! Maybe we can all just take a break and—

No thanks, I don't eat pie made by house-elves.

She is NOT a house-elf!
Gwen, don't listen to them!!
It's okay. I'm used to it now...

You know what, guys? You're not single because of your looks or whatever.
It's because you're **jerks**!!

Oh, I will NOT let someone **"ex-Blaine"** down to me why I'm single!!
"Ex-Blaine" means when a Blaine explains something condescendingly to a Princel.

You don't have to keep explaining every term...

But what am I saying? You're not a Blaine. Look at that sad excuse for a beard.
You'll be joining our club eventually, whether you like it or not.

NOT IF I MURDER ALL OF ITS MEMBERS FIRST!!!

AAAGH!!
Whoa! Saffron, calm down!! This is for Gwen's sake, remember?!

knock
knock
...

Pardon the interruption, ladies and gentlemen.
Your Highness, you asked me to alert you if I noticed any inquisitive villagers.

Well, they're here for you, and they brought weapons.

Villagers? Weapons?! What's going on?!
Um, I see... I'll be right back, everyone. Saffron, can you come with me?
Sure, anything to get me out of here...
We need to take some measures to conceal our identities, though.

See ya later, Stubbles.
AAARGH!!!

And you Princels better be on your best behavior and eat Gwen's pie. **Got it?!**
Gulp
Or else I'll shove my ham hands so far down your throats that you'll never be hungry again.

Shut
Howdy! Do I happen to know you gentlemen?
No, but we're pretty sure we know who you are.
step
step

See, we're sort of the unofficial neighborhood watch. We get a good glimpse of everyone who comes in and out of our little kingdom.
And you seem to match the traits of the infamous female bandit who stole our beloved princess and devastated our people.
Do you know anything about that?

I'm sorry, I don't know what you're referring to.
I am but a humble school teacher, poor yet renowned for her captivating lectures.

Fine. You can try and fake your identity all you want.
And you can try to look inconspicuous with your cloaks and your very generic-looking butler.
Well, that's quite rude...

But you have the exact same horses as our mysterious bandit did when she busted out of here last time.
See, we got a guy who never forgets a horse he's seen once, and he had you pegged the second you rode in.
Yeah, I **REALLY LOVE** horses.

Well, I can't admit to any of the things you're saying.
And I'm sorry if my presence here causes you any pain.

I do regret some horrendous actions from my past.
But the things I've done here aren't one of them.
Oh, you don't bring us any pain, sweetheart. We're gonna get a huge bounty for turning you in.
Fellas, round 'em up dead or alive. We'll worry about getting to the truth later.
crack

You still got some of that pent-up rage, Saffron?
Always.

DASH!
What are you here for this time, you rotten thief?!
SWING
I told you...
SLAM
URGGGH!!
...IT'S EDUCATIONAL!!!

I'm comin' in for backup!!
YIEEEEE!!!
EAT THIS!!!
turn
OW!! Please stop hitting me!!!
SHIING!
Oh, I don't care!! I'll slice right through you **both** for that bounty!!
AAAAH NOOO!!!
OOF!!!

CRACK!
YAAH!!
I wonder how Saffron's doing...
I hate...
HAAAAH!!
...not having...
...A BEARD!!
POW!

Well, that should be enough to hold them off until we leave.

I'll also arrange for the Princels to be relocated so they're not hassled after we're gone.

Not so fast, you stupid b—

CONK
Ah, allow me to arrange the logistics for their relocation, Your Highness.

Why don't I handle cleanup here, so you two can return to check on our other ladies?
Aw thanks, Curtis!

Let's hurry. There's still more I want to discuss with the Princels.
step
step

All right, Princels. I swear, if you said anything—
Swing

hahaha~!

Oh, Gwen, you just make me want to tear down my walls and open myself up to all the joys life has to offer!

Wow...you guys sure warmed up to her!

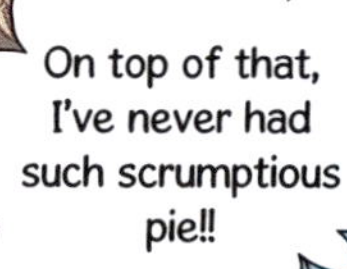
Once you start talking to her, she just makes you feel so special and like you're finally being seen for who you are inside!
On top of that, I've never had such scrumptious pie!!

Gwen, please marry any one of us! Live here in our cottage forever!!!

Oh...! Well, I guess I technically still have a fiancé...
Funny story, it's actually Prince Blaine's brother...!

YOU MONSTER!!
YOU'RE JUST LIKE THE OTHERS!!
HOW DARE YOU TOY WITH OUR HEARTS!!
Uh-oh...
Guys, grab your belongings...
WE HATE YOU!
NEVER SET FOOT HERE AGAIN!
ABORT MISSION! Let's get out of here!!

Chapter
4

step
step

CLANG!
CLATTER
Whoa! What's been going on in here?!

Oh...! W-welcome back, guys!
We all felt anxious while you were gone, so we wanted to help by cleaning the house before you returned.
But then we remembered that none of us are very good at that sort of thing...

I can help with that! I love cleaning!

Ah—not so fast there. We still need to talk, kiddo.
I'm on to you now. You like to help others so you don't have to face your own problems.
grab
But I'm not letting that happen tonight.

Is this place okay, kiddo?

Um, sure...

step

step

tip
toe
Shh...!!
Let's have a seat, then, shall we?

Psst...
Syrah, why are we eavesdropping?
Because!! I didn't take a round trip and let Princels insult me just to miss out on the emotional payoff!

sigh

Gwen, I'm not an expert on curses, but I have lived and experienced quite a bit in life.

And I can tell you fairly confidently that what's been ailing you is not a curse.
It's something else. Something that any person can develop at some point in their lives.

...What **is** it?

Well...
here's my
take on it.

I think that
everyone is born with
a heart that's pure
and unpolluted by the
cruelties that exist
in this world.
But no one
can pass through
life untarnished.

You seemed to have
been sheltered within
your palace walls with
a family who loves you
very, very much.

But when you met Prince Frederick and overheard his words about your appearance...
...that shattered the perception you had of yourself and the world, and it exposed you to the thoughts of shame and comparison that come to all of us.
Gwendolyn is...is... **REALLY UGLY!!!**
REALLY UGLY.
But you repressed those thoughts...
I can't worry about that right now!!!
All I can handle is how to face Frederick and move forward without ruining the engagement for my sisters!!
...which allowed these feelings to breed and grow inside of you unchecked.

And by the time you felt you'd resolved things with your family's engagements, it was too late.
Those feelings had become so strong that they manifested into what you now see in the mirror.

But it's just an **illusion**, Gwen.
You heard what the Princels said when we visited them, right?

A few years ago, I looked in the mirror and saw that I had actual elephant ears growing out of my head.
I just see a potato with glasses.
I see literal trash.
That kind of sounds like what's been happening to me...!

Though that trip was pretty much a bust other than that...
That's right, they did say that. And they're not cursed...

Has this ever happened to you, Prez?

...I've had something similar, yeah...

...When I was younger.

So...if it's an illusion, how do I make it go away?

I feel like if I keep staring into it, I'll find the answer and I'll be able to fix what's wrong with me—

And that's exactly what you **shouldn't** do.
grab

It might seem like the right thing...
but there are some rabbit holes that have no end and will never give you an answer, no matter how long or deeply you stare into them.
And if you keep staring, that broken self-perception will eventually define you and consume the world around you.

But I can't keep ignoring it either!! I thought that's what made it worse!
I don't understand!! What am I supposed to **do,** then?!

Gwen,
all you have
to do...
...is
love yourself.
Exactly the
way you are.

...Love myself?
Exactly like
this...??

I-I'm sorry,
kiddo! I really
should have
brought tissues.

Oh, there's
some right
here!
rustle

...

Rustle
Rustle
Plop!

But until that day, you have to lean more on those of us around you who love you.

And **believe** us when we tell you that you're beautiful.

Okay... I'll try!
And I'm sorry I kept things to myself and made you guys worry about me once again...

Oh, Gwen, you shouldn't be sorry about anything!!

It's Frederick who'll be sorry if we ever get our hands on him...

Guys, you can't all just leave me behind to do the cleaning!
You **know** I'm a hoarder!!!

Sorry, Monika...
We'll all pitch in and help!

Can I help clean too now?
Sigh
Well, okay, only because I think without your help, Curtis will cry when he comes in here.

But make a mental note to do something nice for yourself tomorrow, got it?
Okay, I promise!

...Note...

Wait...!
Prez?
Yes,
kiddo?

I understand that what I've been seeing in the mirror is just an illusion, but...
what about the mysterious notes I've been receiving?

They've been appearing randomly and telling me they can help me become beautiful.
I saved them, but I don't have them on me right now.

Mysterious notes...?

Hmm... Okay, bring them next time.

Hey Gwen, we've got a big cleaning task we need your expertise on!
Oh, sure!

Can we put you in charge of cleaning out our junk cabinet?
It's where all of us stash things when we don't feel like putting them away.
Yeah, I think I can handle that!
Thank you, Gwen!!

Birdseed
Wow, that **is** a lot of junk. Where do I even begin?

Hey, this is from our potion-making night! These are all the wishes that people wrote down about lifting their curse.

I'll start by recycling these scraps.
I don't care about my curse. I wish for a beard and for everyone to compliment my beard
I ♡ wish
Bobby dance

Oh...!!

The next day...
How do I begin to love myself again?
Well, I don't know yet...
But I do know that I always bake for the people I love.
So today, I'll bake for myself.
One hour later...
Oops...I think that's probably enough self-love for one day...
bad at baking in small quantities

I hope it's not a betrayal to myself if I give some brownies to Prez and the CPC.
But I did want to thank them for helping me yet again.

Good afternoon, Prez! I—
step
step

Uh...
grumble

—Oh! ...Hey, kiddo!
Wh-what are you doing here?

Um, I'm just bringing by some extra brownies I made!
Is this a bad time? Everyone seems a little off...

—Oh! Y-you didn't have to come all the way over for that...!!
haha
Well, also... You know how you told me to bring those mysterious notes I received?
I have them here, and I think I figured out where they're coming from—
—I'm sorry, kiddo. Can we put a rain check on this?
I-it's a long story, but I don't feel so hot right now.
Oh, I'm sorry to hear that!! Can I help with anything?
N-no!! You're too sweet. Just, uh, scurry on home and don't come back for about a week,okay?
Club activities are also gonna shut down for a while.
But when you come back, I promise we'll have a big talk about **everything**.

Great! Welp, bye then, kiddo! Have a safe walk home!

Bye, Gwen!!

Uhh, okay! Bye...

Shortly...
I wonder what I should do now that my week has been freed up.
I guess I should probably get started on eating some of these...

Prez and the others were acting kind of weird though...right?

CHOMP!
Oh...! Hey, everyone!
...!
chew~

Because Lance's birthday party is this weekend, and we haven't even received word that Father's coming home.

Not that he'd even let us go in the first place...

sigh~

I can only imagine how fancy and grown-up their birthday parties are.

I bet there's romantic ballroom dancing!!

I bet there are delectable Plaid desserts!!

I bet there're clowns...!!

But we're gonna miss **all** of it!!
I think Daddy deserted us. We're gonna be old maids stuck in this tower forever.
I'm gonna go up to my room to wallow while I glue Schozart back together.

How would you feel about some company and some snacks?
It turns out my extracurricular program is on break.

That actually sounds really nice!
Okay! Let's make a night of it!

Ugggh, what an exhausting trip. Need food before I say hi to the kids—
CREAK...

...FATHER?!

...My babies! A-are those freshly baked brownies?
Just for **me**?!
...
...W-welcome home, Papa...?

Oh, I missed you kids **so much**!!
Papa wants to make it up to you for being gone these last two grueling weeks!!
Hug~
Name anything you want! **Anything at all**!!

Meanwhile, in the not-so-distant Plaid Kingdom...
How come we're **all** being punished with taking care of Laverne...
when that whole harebrained serenade was your idea, Blaine?!

Well, **excuse me** for trying to do something romantic for our fiancés!!
Laverne's treats always look so tasty...

Ah~
Father!!
Shut up and get your work done, idiots.
There's still a lot of prep to be done for the party.

Don't steal from Laverne!!
Here you are, my lady.
SMACK!
Um, Father... have you heard if the Pastel Princesses will be attending?

Aaagh!!
Not yet. This party will be the social event of the season, though, so I do hope they can make it.

I accidentally told my chiropractor the princesses were coming, and he's the biggest gossip around town.
So I'm afraid many people will be expecting their attendance.

THE TARTAN TARTLET

WHAM!
Blaine Fan Club members! We've got an emergency on our hands!
There's a rumor going around that Prince Blaine is **engaged**!!

WHAT??!!! No, that can't be true!!!
Since when?!

Ugh, will you all stop squawking like you're the only ones at this café?
Some of us couldn't care less about Prince **Bland**.
Who could Prince Blaine forsake us for?!

I'm not sure, but it seems like it's an arranged marriage with some puny kingdom.
All the brothers got engaged.
It's also rumored that their new fiancés will be at Lance's birthday party this weekend!

ptoo—
*Did she say **all** the brothers are engaged?!!*

Ladies! Keep your composure.
Haven't we always known that this day would inevitably arrive?
All we can do is be gracious, attend the party...

...and give them a warm welcome to our kingdom.

Chapter 5

Clop
Clop
Clop

I can't believe I was coerced by my smooth-talking children into letting us attend some party at the Plaid Kingdom!
Sigh
I suppose it has been years since I enjoyed a good party with my dear Leland.
And besides that...

...they all look so happy right now.

All right, kids, it seems we have arrived at the palace.
But remember, no matter how exciting things get in there...
you mustn't forget to protect your dignity and keep yourself grounded at all times, okay?
Yes, Father!!!

Wheeee~!!
JACK!!!
YOU MADE
IT!!!!

Sorry we couldn't RSVP properly ! It was a last-minute trip!
Where is your lovely queen, by the way? I brought her some our kingdom's best éclairs!

Why, she's getting dolled up for the party, of course.
!!
Just as you girls shall too— I believe there's enough time!

Oh...Is what we're wearing not suitable for the occasion?

since you're in the Plaid Kingdom...let's get you dressed up in plaid, shall we?

Maids!!

dash–!

It's time for a Plaid makeover!

Trust us, we're experts!

...and into
something much
more worthy of
your beauty!
Oh my!!
I feel like Mrs.
Prince Blaine
already!!!

Where's Gwen?
I can't wait to see how amazing she looks!!
Oh, let me go check on her progress.

Psst! Are you ladies ready to bring out the last princess?
Umm, about that... I-I'm having a bit of trouble with her hair...
How so?

Well, the second I curled it with a hot iron, her hair shrank up and frizzled out.
Hmm, that could be fine. Unruly hair is all the rage these days.

pop!
Actually... there's also a problem with the dress you picked out.
She's a bit scrawny and the dress is kind of swallowing her up.
Okay, well, we can easily tailor things once we take a look at it!

pop!
Makeup's not going so hot either.
Ugh, what now?!

Her skin... It's scaly and oily, like trying to paint a freshwater salmon!
I tried to mattify things with a powder, but I had to use a lot and it's still smudging—

fwoosh—

Ta-da...?

...I'm really thankful for once that I can't see myself...

AHHH, IT'S THE VAMPIRE CLOWN AGAIN!!!!
HOW DID YOU GET HERE AND WHAT HAVE YOU DONE WITH GWEN?!!!

...Wait, Gwen?!
...What the...?

Click
Clack

Snatch
Excuse me...

Pardon my rudeness, but you should be ashamed, calling yourselves experts...
if you can't even properly style someone as naturally gorgeous as Gwen!
Yeah, why would you cover up her face with all this weird stuff?!

—Please, we did the best we could! Don't report us to the king!!
Of course we wouldn't do that over something as trivial as makeup.
We **are** going to take over here, though...

wipe
Gwen, we adore your personal style and all the clothes you make.
But just for today, since we're all trying something different...
will you allow your big sisters to make you up?
Um... sure.

tug~

Okay! Are you ready to step in front of the mirror, Gwen?

M-mirror...?!

...

Don't worry, Gwen.

We think you look gorgeous.
And our style choices are on point, if I do say so myself.

...

Until the day you learn to love yourself...
you have to lean more on those of us around you who love you..
...and **believe** us when we tell you that you're beautiful.

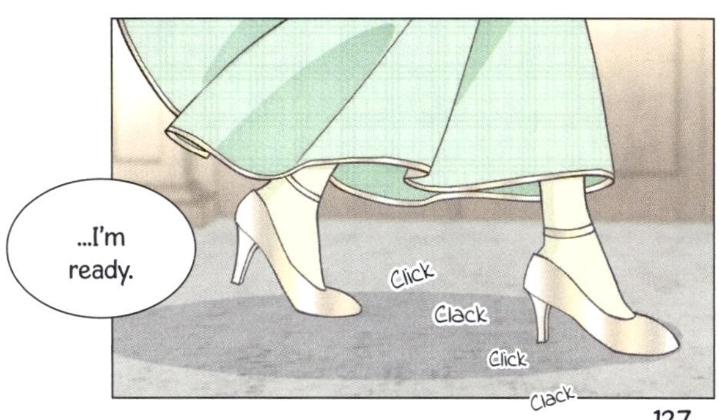

It's...
...IT'S MY FACE!!!!
Heck yeah it's your face, and we love it!!!

Now we just gotta find our way to the grand ballroom!

Well, well, well, if it isn't the Pastel Princesses...

Guess we all cleaned up pretty nicely in plaid!

Happy 20th Birthday
Prince Lance
Chit
Chat
laughter

Blaine!!

Look what my military academy buddies got me—
—a solid gold champagne keg!!
Wanna do a keg stand with me??
Birthday Boy

No thank you, Lance.
I want to keep my wits about me so that I can have very meaningful conversations with Maria and appreciate her on a deeper level.

Whoa, are the Pastel Princesses here?!!
...I haven't seen them. But the night is young, so there's still hope!
BirthDAY Boy

Outside the grand ballroom...
Your Majesty, the horses are being tended to and the birthday gifts have been transported.
Why thank you, Molly.
step
step

Father, wait for us!
Click
Clack

My goodness, you all look beautiful from your makeovers!
Way **too** beautiful...Why would they **do** that?!!

sigh
All right, well, we'll just try to not attract too much attention when we walk into the party.
Let's head on in, everyone.

Your Highness, you left your purse in the carriage, and I figured you may want it this evening.
gasp
I do! Thank you, Molly!!

Ah. Pardon me, but one cannot simply walk into this event.
It is customary for each guest to be announced into the room.

What?!! Announce each of my daughters into that giant room of people?
I've never heard of anything so ridiculous!!
Haven't they participated in a debutante ball where they were presented into society? It's no different than tha—

Present them to society?!! Who would do something so psychotic?!
That's like pointing a giant arrow at my girls and saying, **"Come and get 'em!"**

Psst, Your Majesty, let's not spoil the party by criticizing the customs of other kingdoms.
Hrmph, fine... You may announce us. But don't you **dare** use your outdoor voice...

Your Highnesses, please line up. And when you're announced, just walk in confidently and happily.
Okay!!

Jamie...
tug

I-I'm scared...
I don't want to walk in and have everyone stare at me...

Gwennie...

It'll be okay, Sis. I promise.
Just walk in behind me and stare at the back of my head.
It'll be over before you know it, and you'll realize there's nothing to be scared of, because you're great!

CREAK...
Ladies and gentlemen...
I present to you the royal family...

...of the Pastel Kingdom.
They're here!

gasp
These are the princesses who are rumored to be engaged to the Plaid Princes!!

Hmph, I don't think it's necessary to get so excited over some country bumpkin princesses.
But let's see what they look like...

Did they say the Pastel Kingdom?! I think Prince Blaine is engaged to one of these princesses!
Ugh, we can barely see anything from back here!!!
INSANE FOR BLAINE

Well, it's not like we're guests at this party. We're only here to promote our fan club...
and they stuck our kiosk way over in the back hall.
Shut up! I wanna see this dog who's delusional enough to think she deserves Blaine all to herself.

PLEASE WELCOME PRINCESS M—
Stop it! Stop projecting from your diaphragm!! You're being way too loud!
Mmmph!!
Kids, just walk out really quickly! I'll hold him off!!!

CRASH!!!...

oooh~!!

I'm super proud to be a princess of the Pastel Kingdom!!

...What...?

Having birds and adorable animals from nature appear by your side is one of the irrefutable signs of tremendous beauty!

H-how can someone be so pretty? And where did all those birds come from?!
Is she a sorceress or something?!!
No, you doofus, haven't you ever read a fairy tale?

It's true. I was chased by a wild boar once and I'll never stop bragging to my friends about it.

gasp

Here comes the second Pastel Princess!

...Am I proud to represent our kingdom?

step

step

Blossom~

You bet I am!!!

Whoa, are flowers blooming around her?!

AAAAH MY EYES—!!

It'll be okay, Sis. I promise.

Just walk in behind me and stare at the back of my head.

It'll be over before you know it, and you'll realize there's nothing to be scared of, because you're great!

step step step

Shine~!

I'm proud of our kingdom, but I'm also proud of you, Gwennie!!! You can do this!

This princess is the most radiant of all!!!

applause~

clap

clap

clap

clap~

Jamie was right, this wasn't so scary after all...!
I guess I really do just need to be more confident...

None of the other guests at the party could see for the next five minutes.
Ow, my head.
Didn't see ya there...
Mom...?

...Why is no one clapping for me...?
step
step

To a lifelong friendship!

...Jack? Why are you leaving me hanging?

I'm sorry, Leland. But I can't sit here and not think of all the depravity and violence my children will be exposed to at this party!!

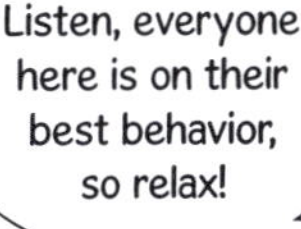

Listen, everyone here is on their best behavior, so relax!
I suggest you start worrying about yourself instead, because the only act of violence will be when I brutally murder you at chess tonight.
Is that so...

Ladies, your entrance was the hit of the party!
And plaid looks fantastic on all of you!!
BirthDAy Boy

We're just so glad we made it here for your gorgeous event tonight!!
Yeah, happy birthday, Lance!! This party is amazing!!
Thank you, Lorena.
BirthDAy Boy

Jamie meant to come greet you as well, but once he locked eyes on the dessert bar, we couldn't tear him away.
The desserts here are pretty great, but nothing can hold a candle to your pie, Gwendolyn.
nod

Thank you!
Um...by the way, where's Frederick?
I feel like we're never at the same place at the same time.

Oh, he hates these parties. He's probably hiding in the library like he always does.
Hey, you should go find him and drag him out here!

Oh! Sure,
I can do that!
Where's your
library?

—Gwen, it's
in the east
wing!
Would you like
to be escorted
there?
That's okay,
I'm sure I'll
find it!

...?
...I
dunno.

step
step
INSANE FOR BLAINE
INSANE FOR BLAINE
INSANE FOR BLAINE
D-do
we have to
do this...?
step

I'm the branch leader of this fan club, which means it's your duty to follow my orders.
And I order you all to find out which one of those Pastel Princesses is engaged to Prince Blaine!!
INSANE FOR BLAINE
INSANE FOR BLAINE
INSANE FOR BLAINE

Well, it's definitely the pink-haired, shiny one.
She was the most beautiful and therefore the one most deserving of Blaine.
...Though they were all ungodly beautiful...
I hate my life.
Okay, then find her!

Molly, help! I can't decide which dessert to try first!
Hurry up, we'll never get a chance to talk to someone as beautiful as her!
I-I know but my legs won't move. I'm so nervous...

SLAM!
OUTTA OUR WAY, LOSERS!!
INSANE FOR BLAINE
WAH!!
There she is. I'm gonna get all up in her perfect face and find out the truth!!
......
U-u-umm, e-e-excuse me...
Wow she's intimidatingly pretty...

OUTTA OUR WAY, GIRLS!!
SHOVE
Normally I'd decline to work during my leisure time, but you caught me when I'm feeling peckish.
So bring on the food!!
Prince Jamie, internationally renowned food critic!!
Rumor spread among our culinary circles that you would be attending the party this evening.
We beg of you, please taste our dishes!!!
ALL HAIL PRINCE JAMIE!!!
However, these formal garments are far too constricting for the job.
So off they come!!
JAMIE, NOOOOO!!! DON'T TAKE OFF YOUR—
fwoosh

...clothes.
Molly, I know not to get naked in other people's kingdoms.
I run a business, you know...
...Did they say prince?
I'm pretty sure the rumors said Blaine was engaged to a princess. So it's not him, then.
But I mean I kinda ship it now...
Well then who—
gasp
There!! That's definitely her!!!
hahaha
Blaine, um... would you like to go to the dance floor?

...Um, as much as I'd love to, I must refuse, Maria.
There's something far more important that I'd really like us to do.
Oh...okay. What could be so important, though?
Maria... I really like you.
And each time we meet, I feel an urge to draw you closer and secure more of your affection.
But I realize now that my acts of devotion have simply been immature and superficial.
So tonight, I want to shed all of that and do something truly intimate to close the gap between us.
...Oh?!
Wh-wh-what do you have in mind...?
He couldn't possibly mean...

Well...
I'd need to take you somewhere where we can be alone for a long time.
It may be uncomfortable at first, but it'll really deepen our relationship and take it to the next level...

R-really??!! You want to do this tonight, Blaine?! Isn't it too soon?
THIS IS THE BEST DAY OF MY LIFE!

I know, but I don't want to wait any longer!! Maria, I—

—I want to spend all night learning about your values and your childhood and your goals in life!!!

...Oh... kayyy...

Ah, I'm so relieved. Let's go, then. I know the perfect place!
step
step

Girls, it's time we carry out the next step in our mission—
SABOTAGE.

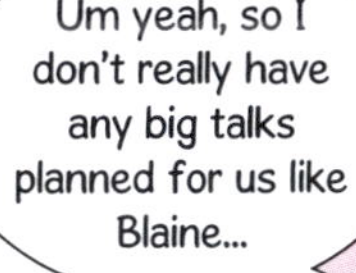

Um yeah, so I don't really have any big talks planned for us like Blaine...
But how do you feel about eating cake and dancing all night?
I like the sound of that!

step
step
Hold it right there...

Happy Birthday, stud.
Oh my gosh, is that...?
I can't believe she's at this party!
Who's that? She looks so cool!!!
That's Suzanna Winchester. She's a big fencing celebrity!!
The Winchesters are a legendary family of fencing champions, and she's only elevated their legacy as their sole daughter.

Hey, Suzanna, it's good to see you again!!

Yes. It's been a long time...
I haven't run into you since...
...since the day that—
—Oh! Where are my manners? Suzanna, meet my fiancé, Lorena!
?!!!

So that's her, huh? She seems like a frail little twit.
...That's quite all right, I don't care to meet—

HIYA!!! Nice to meet you, Suzie!!
I'm really excited to meet a friend of Lance's!
OOF—
SQUEEZE

Do you even **know** who I am?
Because if I were you, I wouldn't feel so comfortable touching me.
WIN CHES TER

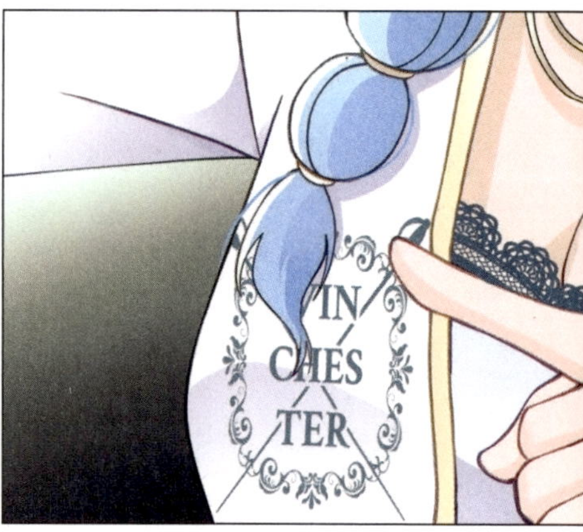
IN CHES TER

"In...ces...ter?"
...I guess you're right. I do feel a little uncomfortable now...

IT SAYS **"WINCHESTER,"** YOU IDIOT!!
Did she just insult my family name??!!

That settles it...

Lorena...
I challenge you to a fight!!

Chapter 6

While Gwendolyn wandered the halls of the Plaid Palace in hopes of finding Frederick in the library...

...the members of the Official Prince Blaine Fan Club were plotting to carry out their mission.

Listen up! We must be discreet and **completely** inculpable!

I don't know what the punishment is for attempting to break up a royal couple, but I sure don't want to find out!!

NOW!!!
pfoo—!

SWOOP

...Did those birds just assist her...?

tsk
Whatever. Task Force B is waiting up ahead for round two.

step
step

I really should have taken Blaine's offer to be escorted to the library...
I'm pretty sure I'm lost now!

Oh, I can ask them for directions!
Why aren't all these sheets folded yet?!
I'm sorry, ma'am! We're short-staffed due to the party!

Squeak~
Well, get it done before I return or you're fired!!
Y-y-yes, ma'am!

Um, excuse me... Would you like some help?

M-miss!! I couldn't possibly allow a guest to fold sheets!!

Oh, it's okay! Our maids let me help all the time!

While Gwen helped fold laundry, Task Force B of the Official Prince Blaine Fan Club lay in wait next door...

SUPPLY CLOSET

Shh! Keep it down, you two!!

I see Prince Blaine and that blond bimbo coming this way.

And she looks unscathed, which means that Task Force A failed and it's up to us.

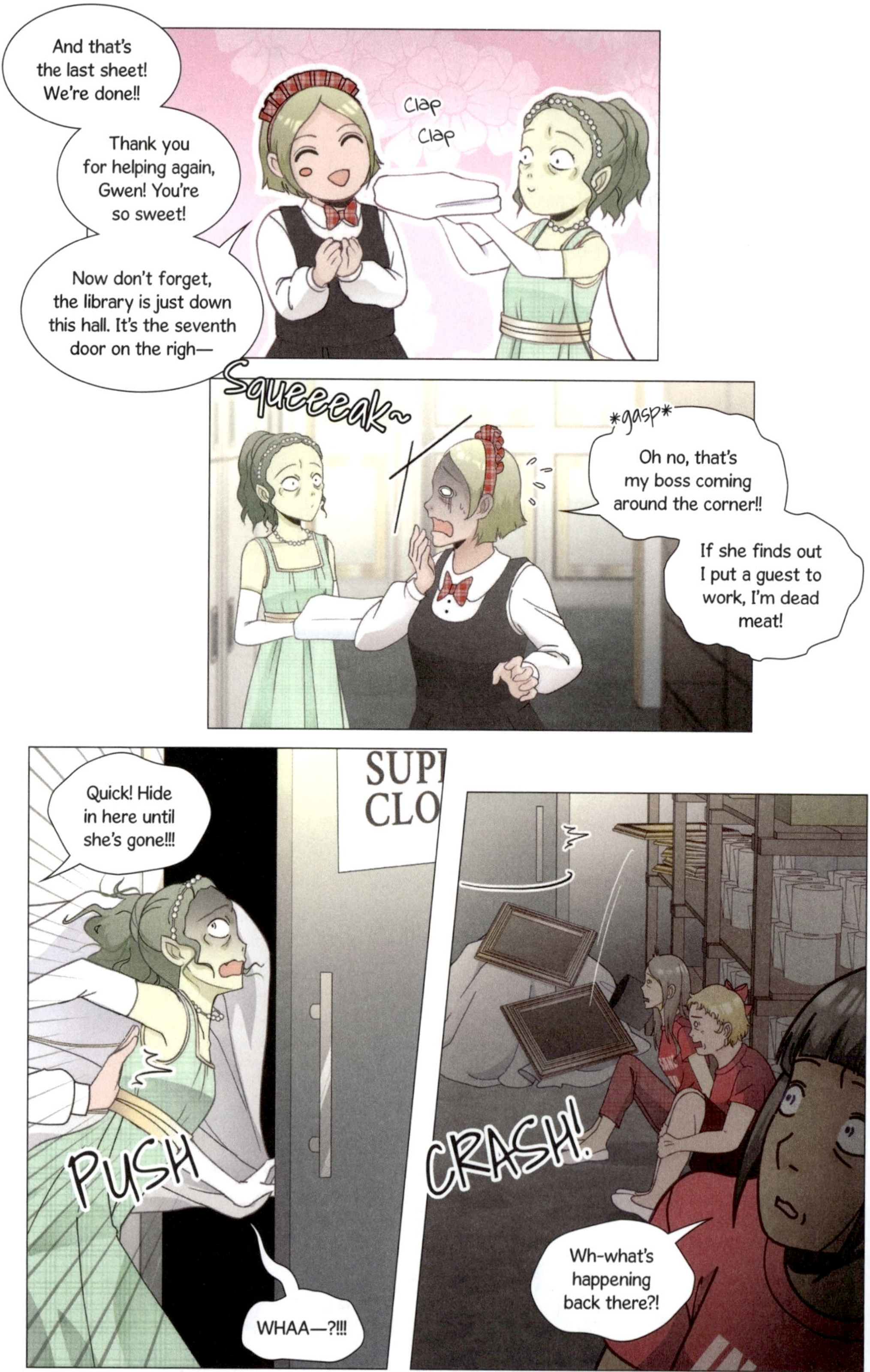

And that's the last sheet! We're done!!
Thank you for helping again, Gwen! You're so sweet!
Now don't forget, the library is just down this hall. It's the seventh door on the righ—
Clap
Clap
Squeeeeak~
gasp
Oh no, that's my boss coming around the corner!!
If she finds out I put a guest to work, I'm dead meat!
SUP
CLO
Quick! Hide in here until she's gone!!!
PUSH
WHAA—?!!!
CRASH!
Wh-what's happening back there?!

S-s-something's moving under that pile of portraits!!!!
I heard rumors that this palace has spirits that haunt their portraits and try to escape through them!!!

Are you kidding me?! It's **obviously** someone from the club trying to scare us!
YANK!
Is it you, Stacy? Is this 'cause I said you had cankles? Huh?!

AGHHH, THANK YOU FOR FREEING ME!!!!

AAAAH!! IT **IS** A HAUNTED PORTRAIT!!!
RUN!!!!

Nooo!!
gasp
IT'S PRINCE BLAINE!!!
Stupid toilet paper—!!!

Oh my, that's unfortunate.

Anyway, I want to hear about all your short and long-term goals in life!
Umm, **all** my goals in life...?! Well...

GRAB
...one of them is to get us back to the party ASAP!!
B-but, Maria!!!

What?! Blaine and his fiancé are headed this way and they're still holding hands!!
Everyone had ONE JOB, and they failed!!!
THE OFFICIAL PRINCE BLAINE FAN CLUB INFORMATIONAL KIOSK

That's all right. It just means that we get the privilege of landing the final blow as soon as she steps through that archway.
And we won't miss... right?
INSANE

Right!

...Is that...

Right on target...

Ooooops!
I'm such a
klutz!!!
TILT

SPLASH!

M-Maria!!!

……

drip
drip

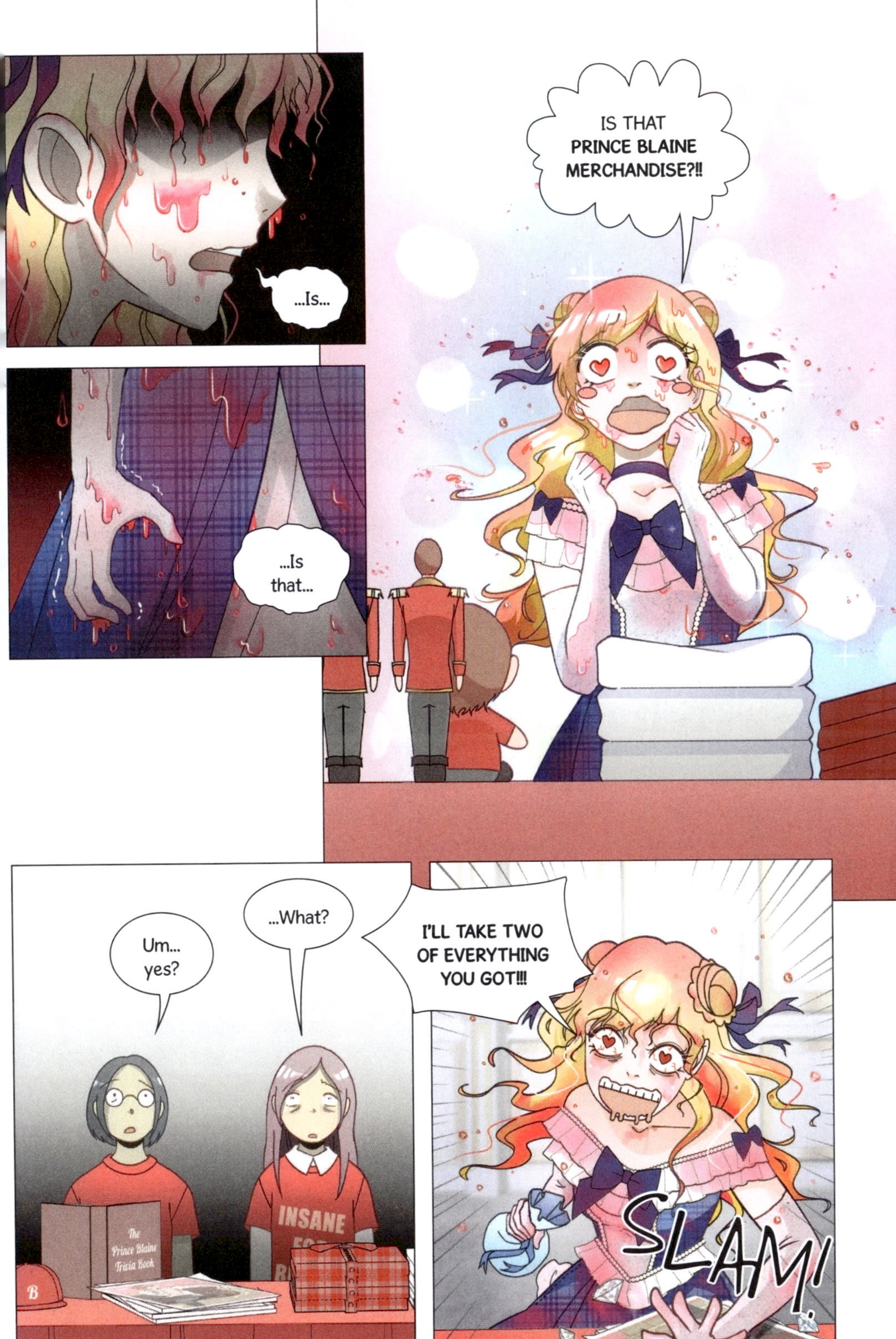
...Is...
...Is that...
IS THAT PRINCE BLAINE MERCHANDISE?!!
Um... yes?
...What?
I'LL TAKE TWO OF EVERYTHING YOU GOT!!!
The Prince Blaine Trivia Book
INSANE
SLAM!

Really?!!
That's gonna be a huge boost for our earnings this quarter!
INSANE

Oh my God, Maria!! Are you okay??!

Am I okay? I'm in heaven right now.
But if you're referring to the fruit punch, well... this is truly who I am, Blaine.
As much as I try to be an elegant princess, I can't seem to suppress the part of me...
that's just an obsessive fan girl with a knack for getting into disgusting messes.
As you may have noticed from the amusement park...

I'm trying to change, but it's hard.
So you don't need to force yourself to improve overnight for me either.
You've been so sweet tonight...
making a genuine effort to learn about me while I've just been trying to dance with you.

...Would you maybe want to meet halfway and continue our talk on the dance floor?
That is, if you're still interested after seeing how atrocious I must look right now.
I just need to find a restroom and clean the punch out of my nose...

Blaine started to realize that he thought Maria looked her most beautiful when she showed her imperfections.

Gulp

I-I would love to.

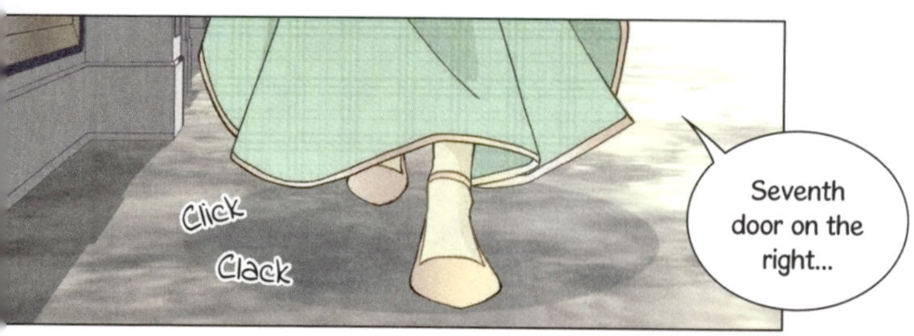
Click
Clack
Seventh door on the right...

Oh, I found it! This is the library!

glance

...Gwen??!

I-I thought that you and your family weren't able to come tonight!
Yeah, we were able to make it just in time.
And Lance mentioned that you might be in the library, so I thought I'd just stop by and say hello.

Um... you can come in...if you want.

...Okay.

...

Um...
...You're dressed a little differently today.

O-oh yeah, it was suggested that we change into plaid for the occasion.
I'm sure it looks really weird—

No.
It's nice...

Umm...oh!! Thank you for lending me your book!
I was entranced by everything from the Angel of Fortune to the giant serpent—
I've never read a fairy tale that was so captivating!

...Really?? I-I'm glad to hear that.
I also realize I never said thank you for the package you sent me.
It meant a lot. Well, mostly the book.
...I'm not really sure what I'm supposed to do with, uh, the other vial.
NEWT EYES
The Little Prawnce

Haha
Ah, I knew I should have shipped a larger bottle! It's probably much more fun when you can get your hands in there, isn't it!

squish~
...I-is that so...

But with the small bottle, I was sort of thinking...

that it could be like a little good luck charm to watch over you.
I-it definitely makes me feel like I'm being watched...

Well, aside from that, this was actually my favorite book when I was younger.
But I... Well, I guess you could say I lost it.
So it was really surprising to see it again.
The Little Prawnce

Oh wow, I had no idea!!
What was it like to read it again?

Yeah, right... They're always surrounded by tons of adoring people, and I'm completely ignored the entire time.

Those parties always make me feel the worst about myself.

Why the heck did I just blurt all of that out right now?!

Um...I've met so many amazing princesses at my extracurricular study. And they've taught me a lot...

They told me that we all need to practice being kind to ourselves every day...
and to listen to the kindness of the people who care about you.

Yeah? What if no one really cares about me...?

Well, that's not true. I care about you.

...

Oh no, I did something totally creepy again, didn't I...??!
stand

...!
I could kind of go for a drink right now.
...Do you wanna go back to the party with me?

Sure, that sounds great!

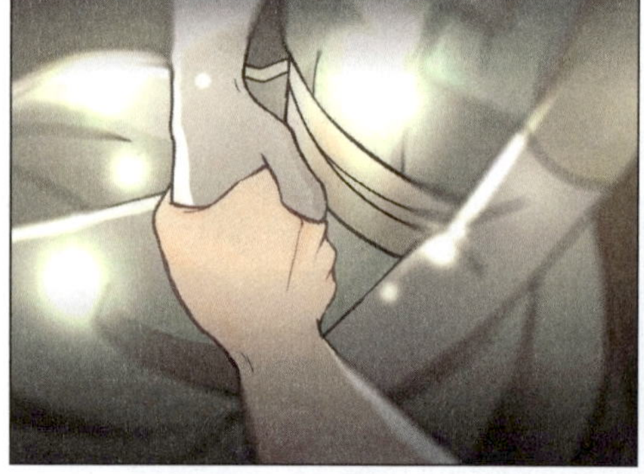

The other day, when she pulled me up from the cliff...
...it was kind of like the book...
Your hand's bleeding!! Gwendolyn, let go!!
No, it's okay! But...I can't lift you up any further...
You'll have to pull yourself up from here...
It's almost as if she's...she's like the—

Frederick...?
—H-huh?!

I-it's nothing! I'm fine!!
Um, how's your hand healing, by the way?
step
step
Oh, it healed really quickly, thanks to your makeshift bandage!
Oh. Good...

Is everything okay?
You seem shocked about something.

What's going on? Why are people in our fencing hall?
Murmur
chatter

Wait...Is that **Lorena**?!!

Your Highness, what have you gotten yourself into?!!

Don't worry, this will just be a fun, quick exhibition match to show what Prince Lance's fiancé is made of...
...because surely anyone who deems themselves worthy of Lance's hand in marriage must at least know her way around a saber!

...Is that what this is?

Uhh, Lorena's never fenced before, has she...?
No. It's not something she was exposed to.
Miss Suzanna is a formidable fencer, I presume?

I don't know. I've never really been into watching women do aggressive sports.
...Didn't you witness Lorena punching out numerous clowns at the amusement park?

Well yeah, but clowns are one thing.
I don't wanna see women attack each other! That makes me kinda sad!!
We're not as fragile as you think, Your Highness.
Perhaps I'm looking forward to this match after all.

I can't believe this dolt agreed to fence when she doesn't even know the first thing about it.
I'm going to thoroughly enjoy humiliating her in front of everyone. Especially Prince Lance.

All right! So let's do a simple five-touch bout, then.
You must remain on the fencing strip, and attacking is allowed anywhere above the waist, including the head.
I hope that's not too scary for you, Princess.

Um, no,
it's okay.
Well then,
let's salute.
Take it away,
referee.

The ref is my
buddy Skippy. He
was on my fencing
team at our military
academy.
He's the one
who got me
a solid gold
champagne keg!
How
charming.

En garde!
Pret!

Allez!!
DASH

YOU NEVER
STOOD A
CHANCE!!!

Wow, at least try to hold your weapon in the right direction.
I'm gonna get her right in the face!!!

POW

HALT! VIOLATION!!!
What? But she said attacks to the head were allowed!

Nooo, with your **sword**, Lorena!!
I take it back. This was a terrible idea...

Oh, Lorena...

NOT WITH YOUR **FIST**, YOU NEANDERTHAL!!
You can only use your sword!
Oooh, my bad...

I'm taking it easy on you and giving you a red card...
mostly because it's very obvious you know nothing about fencing.
But if you do anything illegal like that again, you forfeit the match.
One point is awarded to Suzanna.

WHAT?! I don't need any pity points!!
TAKE IT BACK!

You're talking back to the ref?!
Sigh
Fine, point retracted.
I just wanna go back to playing champagne pong...

Your Highness, you must observe the rules!! Try and watch what Miss Suzanna is doing!
O-okay!

Guess it's time for me to get serious now.

Pret!
Allez!
THRUST!
Whoa!!
Halt! Point awarded to Suzanna!

Halt! Point awarded to Suzanna!
HIT!
AAH—
Another point to Suzanna!
THWACK!
OW!!!
That's more like it.
I can't believe I even challenged this idiot to a fight.

The Plaid Kingdom Fencing Academy for the Gifted and/or Wealthy
I'm the one who gets challenged and targeted by everyone.
As the gorgeous, gifted daughter of one of the most internationally renowned fencing families, I'm used to it.
Clink
Clank
Every girl I meet wants to win against me...
Sniff
Don't worry. Someone's gonna knock her off her pedestal one day, and we'll be living for it.
HIT!
...and every guy I meet simply wants to win me.
AHH!

Suzanna, would you maybe wanna go out for a burger or something—
Ew, gross!
You should be ashamed to grovel for something like that when you can't even beat me in a fight!

But it's fine. I can take them all on and leave everyone in the dust.
FENCING ACAD
As long as they play by the rules...
step
step

step
step

GRAB

SLAM!
OW!! WHAT ARE YOU—?
—Wait, aren't you from my fencing class?
Yeah. You told me I was gross for asking you out without beating you in a fight. Remember?
So what about a fight with real weapons instead of those toy swords?
How does that sound?

step
step
Aww yes, saved the biggest chip for last...
Ah~
chomp
You're nothing but a spoiled, weak little—
Swing
OW!
Hey! Don't butt in here—
CRUNCH

Uh...
I-I mean...
drip
drip
Oh God, did I just cut the face of a Plaid Prince?!

SHOVE
THAT WAS MY LAST CHIP!!!

Pr-Prince Lance...?!

Oh, hey! Have I seen you at the fencing club before?

Um...yeah? I'm Suzanna Winchester.
Cool. Nice to meet you, Suzanna!
Does he not know who I am?! I guess that's a prince for you...

Thanks for the tip. Bye!

...

Y-you don't have anything else you want to say to me...?
Okay, he may not know who I am, but...I mean, I'm still a hot girl he just saved...!
...
Um... I do, actually.
Do you think that chip's still good to eat?
He's not interested in me at all...
Not my looks, not my legacy as a fencer...
I had never met anyone like him. Of course I'd fall in love.

Point awarded to Suzanna!

0 0 0 4

It's been a few years since that happened...

...and I've never been able to get his attention again.

How?!

How can that be, when a memory of our encounter has been physically imprinted on his face?!

Well, I'll finally get his attention again now...

...that I'm about to eviscerate his fiancé right in front of him!

pant pant

Aside from that ridiculous punch at the beginning of the match...
Little Miss Princess was about as pathetic as I could have hoped for.
Crack
But it's time to end things now.

Your Highness! Are you okay? Don't worry, the match is almost over!
I'm okay! I've been watching her like you said, and I think I get it now!

Pret! Allez!
Grip
I just need...

CLANG
...to see my sword as an extension...

...of my fist!!
HIT!
AAH!

Pret! Allez!

HAH!
Whoa, she's getting way too close—I can't use my usual techniques!
step
step
step
She's... she's an infighter?!
HIT!
AAH!
Halt! One point to Princess Lorena!

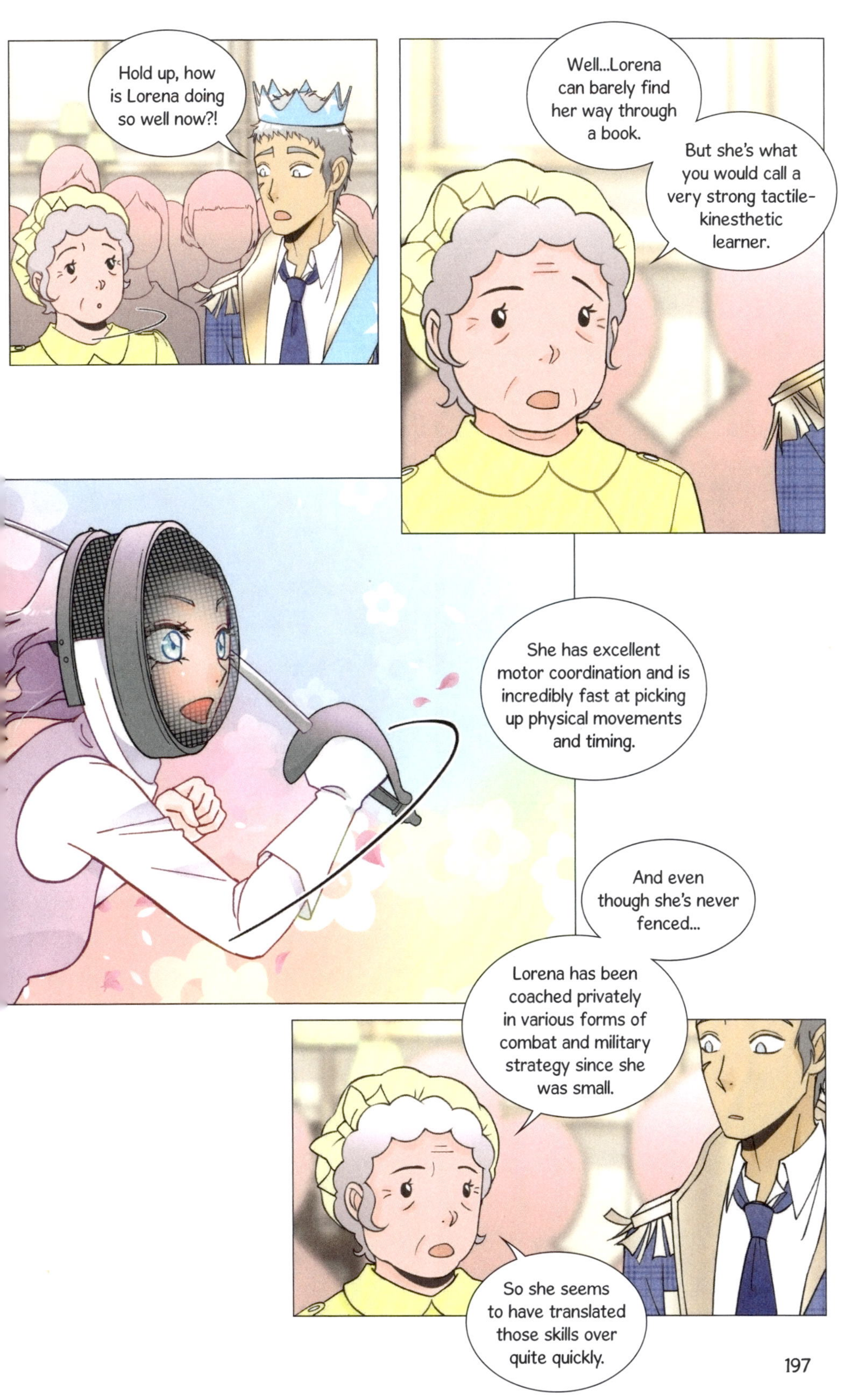
Hold up, how is Lorena doing so well now?!
Well...Lorena can barely find her way through a book.
But she's what you would call a very strong tactile-kinesthetic learner.
She has excellent motor coordination and is incredibly fast at picking up physical movements and timing.
And even though she's never fenced...
Lorena has been coached privately in various forms of combat and military strategy since she was small.
So she seems to have translated those skills over quite quickly.

Due to the king's rule of keeping them cloistered within the palace walls...

the Pastel Princesses have missed out on learning a lot of the social norms that come from interacting with their peers and society.

But they've taken that time to engross themselves in countless hours of practice in their individual passions.

0 4 0 4
Another point to Princess Lorena!
Pant
I-it's down to the final point?!
I can't possibly lose to some idiotic brute who's never held a sword before!

SLAP!
COME ON, SUZANNA! THIS MATCH BELONGS TO YOU!
YOU'RE A WINCHESTER NOT A LOSECHESTER!!

It's the final point, and it's anyone's match!
I'm proud of you, Lorena! Keep it up!!
Clap
Clap
BirthDAY Boy

En garde!
Pret!
Allez!

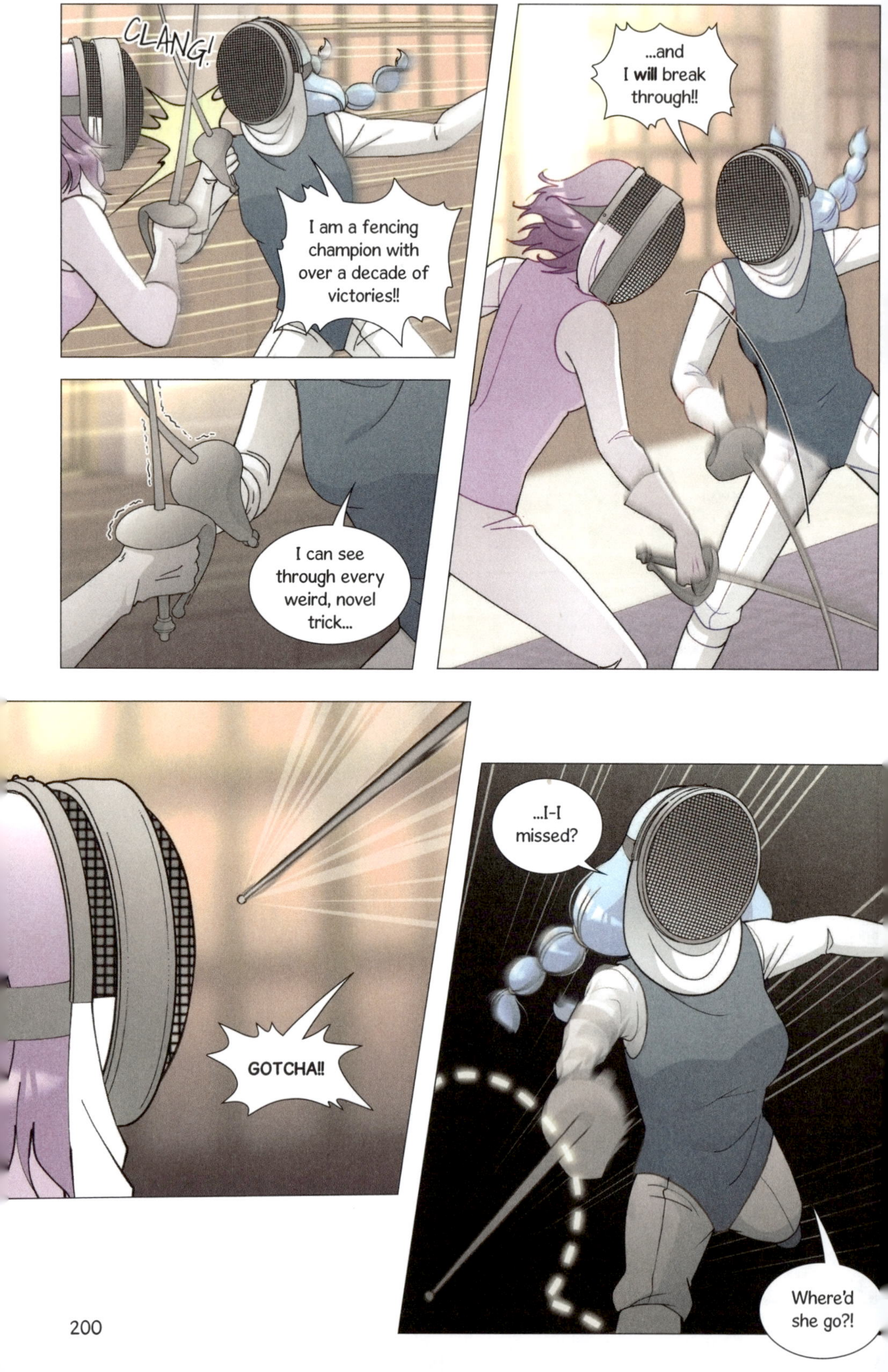

CLANG!

I am a fencing champion with over a decade of victories!!

I can see through every weird, novel trick...

...and I **will** break through!!

GOTCHA!!

...I-I missed?

Where'd she go?!

ZOOM!!
NO... NOOOO!!!
STOP
...Huh?
Whoa, that was close!
I forgot what we were playing for a second. I'm not supposed to kick!
...

Well, that was a little anticlimactic... But whatever. I won fair and square.

AGHHH—!!

Let's see how she's taking the loss in front of everyone. Is she humiliated?

I love it when they ugly cry.

Hug~

Lance! What the heck was that?!

tap

After that day, Lance became a lifelong supporter of women's combat sports.

I KNOW, RIGHT?!

That was the most **AWESOME** birthday present of my life!!

Lift

WOMEN'S FENCING RULES!!

BirthDAY Boy

Cheers to that!

Um, should we head back to the party as well?

Okay!

step

step

RRRUMBLE!!!...
TO THE KEG!!!
AAH—!
grab

JEEZ!! Watch where you're going, you meatheads!!
stomp stomp!
Ugh, let's walk as far away from them as possible.

...S-sure...

Chapter
7

munch
munch

Oh...?

step
step
What do we have here?

I'll go and get us two glasses of punch.
Great! Then I'll grab us that table over there.

Very niiiice,
Gwennie.

Um...
Prince Jamie?
Wh-what are your
thoughts on my
carbonara?

What?
—Oh, right!
Uh, the texture of
the sauce is rich
and velvety,
but it's being
weighed down
by your fear of your
coworkers finding
out about your full-
body rash.

...!!
I-I mean—!
Crap, sorry
about that...

I'm having a really nice time at this party. But I honestly wouldn't mind sitting down for a while!
step
step
I'm also excited to get to talk more with Frederick...

!!
Here's a seat, babe!
Nice find, babe.
—Oh!! I guess I was too slow. ...What should I do now?

SMOOCH~
Umm, I-I'll just stand and face this way until Frederick comes back, so we can find a new table together...

SCOOP

Oh my, is this little Frederick?
tap

Wow...look at you!
Oh my, you're so grown-up now!

I know these girls. They're always at these parties clinging to Blaine and Lance.
Why are they talking to me all of a sudden?

Why haven't you been at these functions all these years?

I've been here. It's just that no one noticed me...

Uh-huh...
turn
I need to get these drinks back to Gwen...

Oh. Well we're certainly noticing you now, and we like what we see!

I mean it! I feel like I'm seeing you in a whole new light.
I agree, I think Blaine and Lance need to watch out for you now...!

How long have I dreamed...
of the day where I'd finally be seen by the people who have always ignored me?

It's finally happening now...
So why does it feel so... unpleasant?
And yet...

...why do I want to hear them say more?
So what have you been up to all these years?
Gwen's waiting for you...

We wanna hear all about you, Frederick.
droop...
Just a little longer...

There must be a long line at the punch bar...
Smooch Smooch
I'd go find him, but I think I should stay put so we don't cross each other's paths in this giant ballroom.

Oh, maybe I can find him if I just keep looking around...

It's great to see you again!
You too!

Another glass of merlot please, Bart.
Hmm.. No, I don't see him.

Oh!! I think that's him over there!

Hahaha. Oh Frederick! You're funny too!

...!!

He...
...He looks like he's having a nice conversation with people.

I don't want to interrupt...
...especially since he said he never has a good time at these parties...

I've never been in a room with so many people before...
chatter
chatter

And yet somehow... I've never felt more lonely...

Gwennie! Hey, Gwen!!

Darn it, she's too far away to hear me, and she won't look over in this direction for some reason.
Why's she standing alone still? Where did Frederick go?!
Chomp

I can't leave because this is the last batch of chefs I promised to critique.
But Gwennie really looks like she could use some company!

I know!! Maybe if I give more brutally honest reviews, everyone will leave in protest!
It's...It's completely inadequate!!
Prince Jamie, how is my baba ghanoush?
You need to salt the eggplant and draw out the bitterness,
along with your secret infatuation for your sommelier!!!

SMOOCH
SMOOOCH

Oops. Sorry, Gwennie.

I'm so bored, Bart. Aren't you?
Yes, My Lord.

I came tonight to find inspiration. But how can I when everyone here is just so—

Wait. Who is that...?!

Sooo, Frederick, do you feel like coming up to the lodge with us this fall?
It's gonna be so much fun!

Um, well...
Isn't this the opportunity I've been waiting for...?
To be lifted out of the hole I've been stuck in for so long?
I can't let this chance slip away...right?
So why am I hesitating...?

Whoa. Check out that girl with the green hair and green plaid dress.
Hahaha, oh **wow**...

YEAH?! WHAT **ABOUT** HER??!!!
...!!

Uhh...I was just saying, "Check out that girl. She's totally getting hit on by that dude."

—Wait, **what**?!!

Please, tell me your name...
...because you are absolutely beautiful.

...!!
I mean, I think he needs his eyes checked, though...
Hahaha.

So what do you say, Frederick? Will you come to the lodge with us?

No. I actually couldn't be less interested.

step
step
step

Um, my name?
I-I'm Princess Gwendolyn of the Pastel Kingdom.

...of the **Pastel Kingdom**?
Hmm, that's odd. I don't recall seeing you enter the party with the rest of your family...

Well anyhow, my name is Lord Leopold of the Argyle Kingdom.
It's simply a courtesy title, though. I'm a mere painter at heart, and nothing bores me more than these sterile parties.
I saw you standing here from afar and couldn't help but think that you might be feeling the same way.

I-I'm really sorry I took so long...
pant
Um, it's okay...!

Oh, I apologize! I didn't know you were accompanied by a date.
I had been observing the party for a while from the balcony.

I saw Gwendolyn standing quite alone...
while I believe I saw you having a very fun time chatting up multiple women at the punch table.

...
N-no! I—
It wasn't fun...

But, I'm not so much of a scoundrel as to steal a woman away whilst she's on a date...
regardless of the quality.

—Oh!
Hold on
there!
I didn't recognize
you without your
plaid jacket, but you're
Prince Frederick,
aren't you?
My cousin is
Prince Griffin of
the Argyle
Kingdom!
I met you when your
brother Blaine competed
against him at the finals
of the Inter-Kingdom
Piano Showcase,
remember?

How could I get
second place to that
heavy-handed lummox!!
Those judges have
no taste!!
2nd
Oh...
right...

Wait...Does
that mean the
rumors are true?
Are you going to
marry Princess
Gwendolyn?

HUH?!!!
—W-well,
umm...

No.

Don't worry, Frederick. It's okay.
I haven't forgotten what we talked about in the hallway of our palace about just being friends.

Huh...?! What are you talking about? When did we—?

...!!
gasp

LET'S BE FRIENDS, FREDERICK.
FROM NOW ON, I'LL BE WATCHING YOU FROM THE SHADOWS.
I HOPE YOU'RE HAPPY...

Wait...so that was all **sincere**?!
Wh-what else have I been misunderstanding, then...?

Oh!! You're just friends? Why, that's wonderful news! In that case...

...would you like to come with me, Gwendolyn?

I-I'm so confused about everything right now...
But I feel like I don't want her to walk away with him...

I also feel like I have no right to stop her, though...
I can't do anything...

SMACK!
HEY!!

I saw that, Leopold!
How dare you interfere with my brother and his dear fiancé?!

Blaine...!!
He stood up for me?

You're just like your cousin, taking precious things that don't belong to you!!
Now shoo!
Hi, Gwen!! You been having fun tonight?
Um, y-yeah...

And you!
Listen, I know you despise it when I try to give you advice, but...

...if there's something you really want, you have to **go after it**, Frederick!!

...

Hey, Cuz. Oh hi there, Blainey!!
Oh no...
If it isn't the prince of the Argyle Kingdom...
Haven't seen you at the competitions this year!
You still dabble at the keys?
I've been busy...!!
Wow, this must be your fiancé!!
My name's Prince Griffin. My hands can reach a thirteenth on the piano.
Wanna feel?
hahaha
That's **obscene**!! No one needs to reach a thirteenth!!!
Blaine, why don't we just go dance?
STOP LAUGHING!!! You look like a big sock!!
Um, okay...
Why don't I just go get us some cake first...

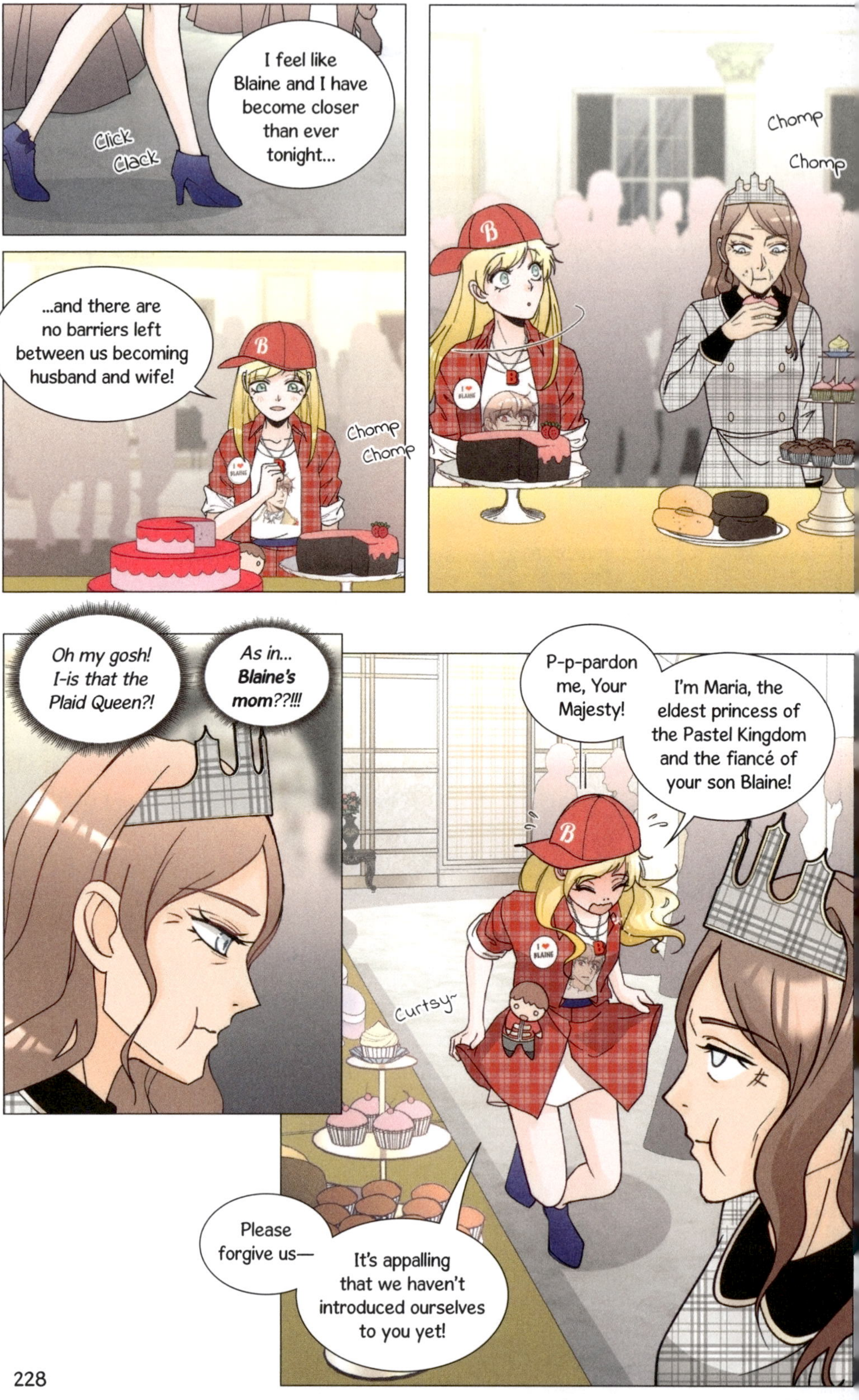

Oh my gosh! I-is that the Plaid Queen?!

*As in... **Blaine's mom**??!!!*

P-p-pardon me, Your Majesty!

I'm Maria, the eldest princess of the Pastel Kingdom and the fiancé of your son Blaine!

Curtsy~

Please forgive us—

It's appalling that we haven't introduced ourselves to you yet!

Oh.
No, it's not appalling.
That's very kind of you to say, Your Majesty—

I kept it that way...
because I don't want any of you here.
I don't approve of any of this arranged nonsense.

Wh-what...?

Please, wait!!
It may have been arranged, b-but it's not nonsense!
I **really** love Blaine!!!

...Uh, yeah.
I could tell from your... **merch**.

step
step

Sigh
I apologize for my unsightly outburst earlier when I chased off the Argyle Prince and his cousin.
But I couldn't help it— They just have no sense of tact or proper etiquette!

Take their hideous taste in neckwear, for example.
A neckerchief at an evening function?! I couldn't possibly...
...

If there's something you really want, you have to **go after it**, Frederick!!

Something I want...?
What is it...
...that I really want?

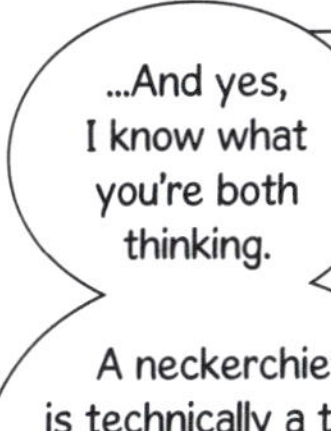
...And yes,
I know what
you're both
thinking.

A neckerchief
is technically a type
of cravat, as are
ascots and neckties,
but—
Oh! There you
are, Maria. Shall
we have that
dance now?
step
step

?
Nah, I'm
good.

Hey, guys!! I
want you to meet
my new best
friend, Suzie!
WE'RE NOT
FRIENDS!!

Hahaha...

EVERYONE, LOOK OVER HERE!!

GONG!

Wooooo!

Yeaaah!

It's time for everyone to cheer on the birthday boy as he does a midnight keg stand!!

Um, while this is generally how all our functions end,
Father seems particularly annoyed this time.
Oh, that would be my fault.
I accidentally lost track of time going on a chess bender with your pops tonight.
And I had a **savage** winning streak.

Excuse me, pardon me...
Thank goodness the party's over and all the chefs finally left!
I need to get to Gwen!

Ah, there she is!
Gwennie, what happened? Is everything okay?!

Stop
Um, this was a fun party!
Your palace's functions are definitely a lot more eventful than ours.

All right, kids! Papa kept his word and let you all attend the party.

But we need to go! It's way past all of your bedtimes!

SWOOP!

And so the Pastel King wrangled everyone to the exit to make their way back home.

But they couldn't bear to leave without picking up a few souvenirs and commemorative portraits.

GET A PORTRAIT WITH LAVERNE

Maria, Lorena... what are you wearing...?!

Chapter 8

The next day, back in the Pastel Kingdom...

step
step
Prez told me last time to wait a week before I returned to the CPC.
It's a little earlier than that, but I just can't wait to see everyone.

I hope she's feeling better.
I brought her some hot soup just in case!

I think Abbi will be excited to hear that Frederick liked the gifts we got when we went shopping!

And I think Prez will be really happy to hear that...
I saw my face in the mirror again, thanks to her advice and my sisters.

But, then later...
when I was standing alone at the party...
...it was almost as if I could feel the cracks returning to my face...

I don't really understand it at all, but...

self-love seems like a hard thing to hold on to.

step

step

rustle

No one's
here either,
huh?

Well, I'll just
go drop these
off in the
kitchen!

step

step

KEEP CALM AND P.A.N.D.A.

LOVE YOURSELF

Well, the souvenirs have been dropped off, so I guess I'll head home now—

Is that another note...?!
To Gwen

...H-hello? Is someone here?
I must have missed them when I walked to the kitchen...

"It's time. Meet me tonight at midnight...
inside the red building at the south end of the forest."

Meet me tonight
inside the red
the south end of
ake you beautiful.
"I will make you beautiful."

I'll go tonight and tell them in person that I appreciate their concern,

but they don't need to worry about me anymore.

step

step

Hmm, it's almost midnight,

but I haven't been able to find a red building yet.

I wish we could have spoken face to face at the CPC headquarters...

instead of meeting out here like this.

But it's okay. The least I can do is properly explain things to them.

But a lot has changed since then.
And even though I still don't have it fully down yet...
I think I have all the answers I need for now.

And if it's a makeover they have planned for me...
I think I've had enough of those for a while too...
step
step

Oh! There it is!!

step
step

Hello?
knock
knock
The note said to meet inside, right?

Oh, the door's unlocked...
push
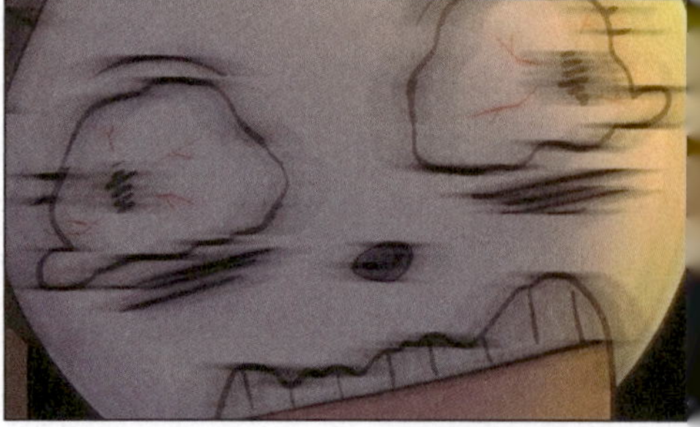

CREEEAK...
Hello?
Is anyone
here?

I can barely
see anything in
front of me...
step
step

scratch
scratch

O-oh...!!

Umm...

A-are you here to make me beautiful?

JUMP

AAAHHH!!

Maybe I came to the wrong place...
Either way, I need to get out of here.
Tic
Tic
Tic
Except... it's blocking the door!!
I-it's okay, it's just a spider! I see them all the time in my room and in our palace...!
And it should be no different than what I say to Maria anytime she's scared of them...
They don't want to hurt us!
They're much more scared of us than we are of them!
Then I put a cup over the spider, and I let it out a window on the ground floor.
plop
M-maybe that could work here...!

Oh, and there's a cup! I'll just grab it and—
tic
tic
tic

—!!
STAB!

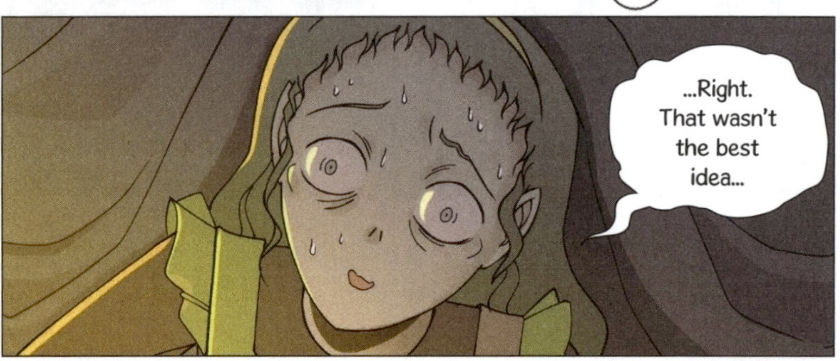
...Right. That wasn't the best idea...

Wait a second...
Aren't those the brownies I brought a few days ago?
Is this someone's room?

Maybe the spider accidentally wandered in through that window.
It looks like it's locked, though...

Well, they do seem to somehow fit through even the smallest cracks.
Hello~!

So I'll just sneak over...

creak
...and open up these shutters...
and I'm sure the spider will be excited to get out and return to its habitat!

tic
tic
tic
tic
tic
tic

It's working!!

tic
tic
tic
N-no, spider! Don't run toward me...
Go toward the window!!
SHRIEK!!
AAAAH!!

POW!
SLAM!
Curtis?!!
My goodness, What have I done...?
C-come with me, Miss Gwendolyn!!

WE NEED TO GET OUT OF HERE!!

SHUT

...!!

Miss Gwendolyn, are you hurt anywhere?!
pant
pant

No, I'm fine, Curtis.
But what was—?

Curtis?
Gwen?!
...?

Wh-what's going on out here?!

I'm so sorry I woke everyone up!!
I went into this building and a giant spider was in there.
But it's okay! Curtis saved me.

Did she say...
Gasp
..."Spider"?!

Ohhh, I get it. G-giant spider, huh...?
I guess it's time for me to step it up as the dude of the group.
Y-y-you ladies can leave it to me...

I'm just gonna put on some protective gear, grab a blow torch...
and when I come back, we'll burn the whole place down real quick!
I'll be right back...!!
dash~!

Banished from the Cursed Princes Club... **forever**?!
But I don't want to leave...
There's so much more I want to do with them...
What have I done...?!
How did I not realize I was in the barn?!

Wait, everyone! We still haven't heard from Gwen yet!
I'm sure she has a good reason she was in the barn!!

Why were you in there, Gwen?
Um, w-well...there are these notes that mysteriously show up in my pocket...
a-and they say they want to help me, and...

That sounds like what I said when I got caught cheating on my math test...
Huh...?
I tried, Gwen!! I'm gonna really miss you!!

I-I have them here if you'd like to see.
Prez wanted me to show them to her...
so I've been keeping them in my bag.

Whoa...you were actually serious about that?!
grab

Gwen, these are **terrifying**!
It's sort of like... you were being set up by someone to wander into the barn...
To Gwen

...Someone who knows our club's commandments and wanted to cause you harm.
But who could ever do something like that?
Especially to you, of all people?
Everyone loves you...

W-well, I don't think they meant me any harm—

gasp
NOT EVERYONE LOVES GWEN!!
Not Nell, I saw her!!
She wouldn't stop glaring at Gwen during the slumber party **and** when we had lectures!!

Nell??!!
How could you?!!
That's really awful, Nell!!!
HISSSS!!

W-wait!

I can say with utmost certainty that it was not Nell.
...

She happened to spot Gwen walking through the forest and became apprehensive about where she was headed.

Being too terrified to approach the barn herself...
she ran and notified me as fast as she could.

It's all thanks to Nell that Gwen made it out safely.
Oops... Sorry, Nell...
It's okay.

Nell saved me??

Besides, it seems like Miss Gwendolyn already knows who sent her those notes.
Is that correct?

Gwen, is that true? You know who it was?!
You need to tell us!!
W-well, I really don't know for sure!
But it kind of seemed like the person who sent them was...

...Aurelia.

What...?!
How could you accuse me of something like that, Gwen??!
I've only talked to you once before...
but I thought you were nice and we could become better friends!!

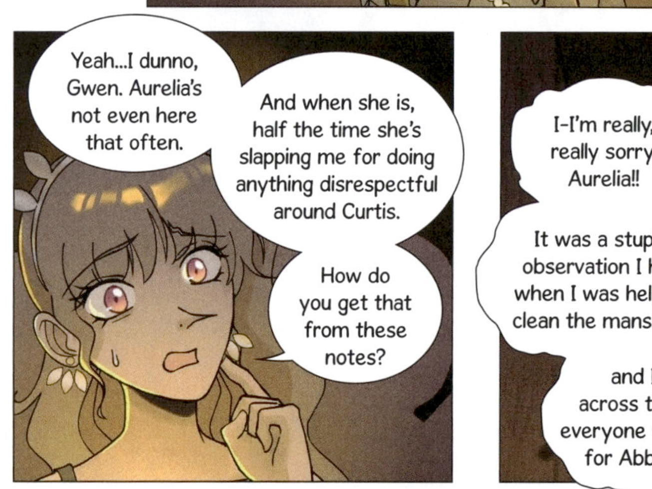
Yeah...I dunno, Gwen. Aurelia's not even here that often.
And when she is, half the time she's slapping me for doing anything disrespectful around Curtis.
How do you get that from these notes?

I-I'm really, really sorry, Aurelia!!
It was a stupid observation I had when I was helping clean the mansion...
and I came across the wishes everyone wrote down for Abbi's potion.

Everyone was supposed to think of something they desired if they didn't have their curse...
and jot it down on a piece of paper.
But one of the pieces of paper caught my eye...
because the handwriting matched the notes I had been receiving.

Really? What did it say?
Huh? Oh...
I-it said they wanted to experience their first kiss. But—

Really?!
That was your logic for accusing me?!
I mean, that's like everyone here! We're all a bunch of rejected, virgin princesses!!

Pfft, speak for yourself, sister.

I-it wasn't so much what the note said...
rustle

In the instructions for Abbi's potion...
everyone was supposed to kiss the paper to activate the spell...

But this one had disintegrated the paper where the kiss was.
And the only person I knew who could do that was...
I want to have my first kiss

...Aurelia.

The handwriting **does** match exactly.
The biggest question I have, though, is...

...why do you have such creepy handwriting, Aurelia?

I regret everything about that whole potion experience...
But whatever!!
Just because you're shaming my penmanship, it doesn't mean anything—

Hmm, that would account for something I observed as well.
I had been wondering how Miss Gwendolyn broke through the numerous locks on the barn.

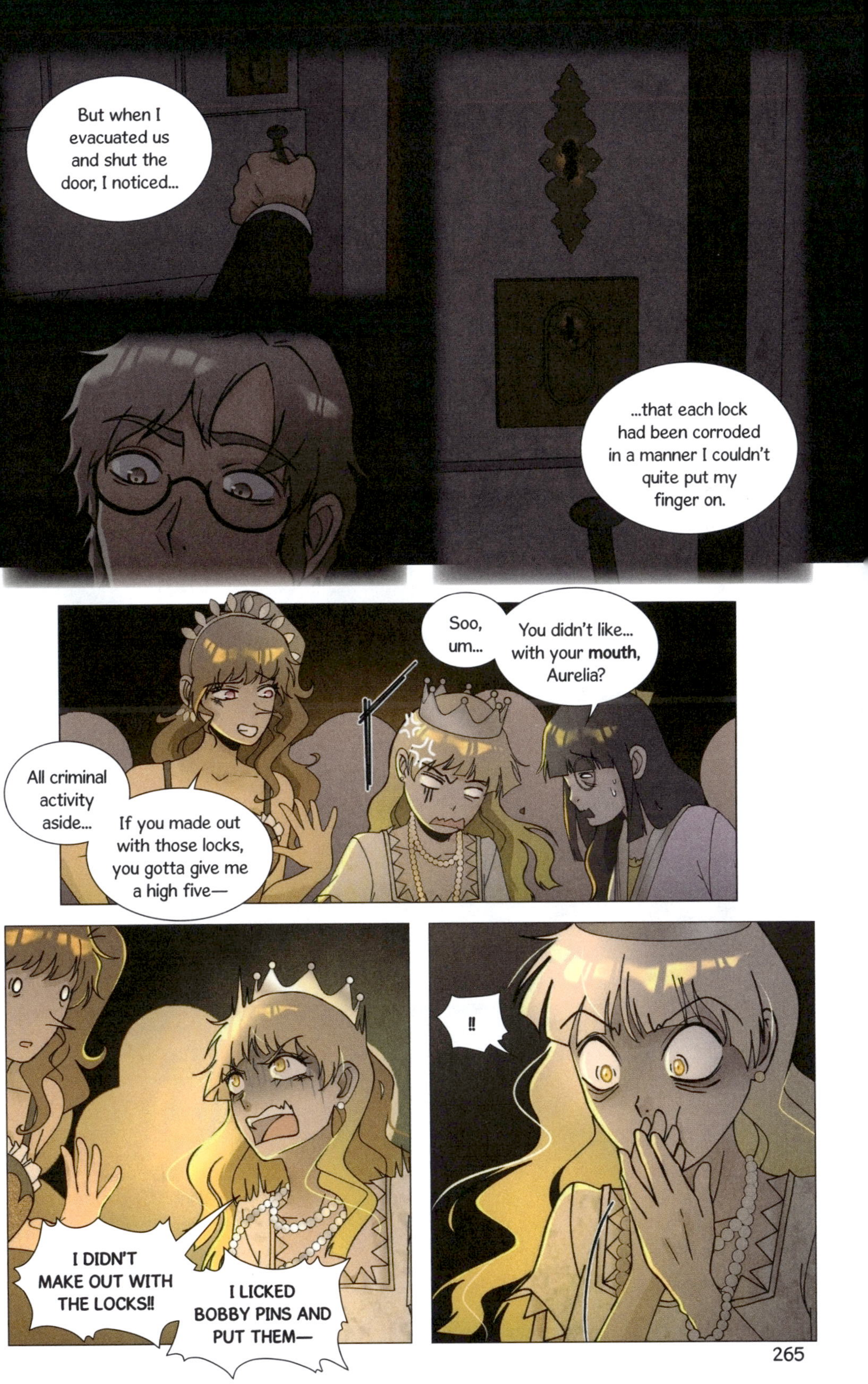

But when I evacuated us and shut the door, I noticed...

...that each lock had been corroded in a manner I couldn't quite put my finger on.

I was the one who wrote the notes...

and dropped them when no one was looking...

Someone help, I'm stuck...

...or when Gwen wasn't around.

Leave?! But why don't you want Gwen in our club?
Why...? Because...
...SHE'S NOT CURSED!!
So why do we all continue to let her come here??!
shake
You have all these other princesses who've been relegated to the back of the club.
They should be getting the spotlight, not her!!
Um no, I'm all right...
I don't really like a lot of attention...
But no, Gwen constantly gets advice and special parties...
and she gets to decide lecture themes—
...Is that really a perk, though...?

The point is that she doesn't belong here.
SHE'S NOT CURSED.
SHE'S JUST UGLY!!!!
Whoa! Hold up—
Gwen!! You already have everything— a fiancé, a loving family...
So you wanna know how to become beautiful?!
All you have to do is grow out your bangs...
put on some heavy makeup...
and stop sewing toddler clothes for yourself!!!

HEY!
Get away from Gwen!!
A-and some of us like her toddler clothes, you know...

...!!

CREEAK
step
step
step

Just help yourself for once, Gwen!!
I know Prez leaps at every opportunity to fix things for you with a long talk and a group hug.
But guess what? She's not here now!!
So just go back home and—
tap
Sorry to interrupt, but...
...did someone say "group hug"?

P-Prez...!
Hey there, kiddo. Would you mind leaving the two of us to have a little chat?
Why don't you join the rest of your clubmates?
Um, o-okay...
stumble
Gwen, get over here! Quickly!!
The rest of my clubmates...?

Gwen, don't listen to what Aurelia said!
You heard Prez. You're a club member and don't ever forget it!!

Really...? I get to stay in the club?!

But...what about...?

Aurelia...
step
SLAM!
!!!
You have **no idea** how angry I am about what you did to Gwen.

I-I'm sorry for what I did, but I stand by what I said!
Gwen doesn't belong in the Cursed Princess Club!
She doesn't even fulfill the fundamental rule of being cursed!!

It's never been a commandment that someone needs to be cursed to be in the Cursed Princess Club.
But you know what **is**?

"Assisting others."
PANDA

And you violated that by purposefully putting Gwen in harm's way...
...and tricking her into going into the barn.

Y-you heard that? When did you get here...?!

What do you mean? I was here the entire time...
...in the barn.

What?! No you weren't!!
They said there was a giant spider in there that—

GASP!

What...?
In the barn...? Th-that was...

Don't go anywhere near the barn.
Just, uh, scurry on home and don't come back for about a week, okay?
No... it couldn't have been...!

You can't do this!!
I promise you'll regret it!!

I'm really sorry, Aurelia.
This isn't a decision I enjoy making.
But I must give you this warning.
TIC
TIC
TIC

Don't even think of trying to do anything to expose or harm this club...
because from now on, they'll always be keeping their eyes on you.

And they tell me everything.

SNAP
AAAAH!!

You have until sundown today to be out of the forest.
step
step

ptoo!

...

...Fine.
See ya.
step
step

Sooo, does anyone wanna play charades or something?
I don't think I can go back to sleep right now...

Well, I don't think I can ever sleep again...
until Nell forgives me for accusing her of glaring at Gwen!!
H-huh?! I said it was fine...

No! It's not fine!!
I totally wasn't thinking about your curse!
You haven't been glaring at Gwen this whole time—You've been trying to **warn** her!!

Warn me...?

Ohhh, of course!!
You're such a sweetie, Nell!

What?! No!!
I WAS glaring at Gwen!
Because she's always clinging to Jolie...
...and I don't like when people put their hands on my girlfriend!
—I'm sorry. Can you say that again?
...
Nell!! I thought you wanted to keep things quiet!
I didn't mean to make you jealous. You should have told me!
C-clinging?! When did I—?

You're a little home-wrecker, Gwen.
I-I really didn't mean to...!

Wait! Nell, can I ask what your curse is?

dash~
...

HISSSSS!!

I'm gonna go after her.
I think we'll have to let her tell you about her curse some other night, Gwen.
Oh, that's fine...!

Perhaps you'll settle for hearing about my curse tonight?

...R-really?

It's the very least I owe you after everything that's happened.

All right, everyone, take a seat and be quiet!
Prez doesn't tell this story often, so you don't wanna miss it!!
Curtis, can we get some popcorn, please?

OKAY, EVERYONE, I'M BACK!
dash
And I'm ready to squash that stupid spider! Where is it?!

Just sit down, Saffron.

Everyone in the Cursed Princess Club sat in silence, eager to hear the story of Prez's curse.

This included those who had never heard the story before...

...as well as those who already knew it well.

Gwen, I'm really sorry for not telling you about my curse sooner.
I meant to, but...it's not an easy story for me to tell.
So here we go...

Chapter 9

WARNING

This chapter contains
some blood and violence.
Viewer discretion is advised.

This story begins in my home of the Polygon Kingdom.

My parents were endlessly pleased that I turned out to be everything I was supposed to be—Smart, obedient, and easy on the eyes.

For these were traits that would attract many eager suitors.

After much vetting, it was decided that on my 21st birthday I would marry the eldest prince of the lavishly powerful Monochrome Kingdom.
Darling Calpernia, you've always excelled at everything we've asked of you.
Now it is time for the most important task of your life. Can you do this for us and for your kingdom?
...
...Yes, Mother. Yes, Father.
As I grew older, I began to feel more and more unwell, for some reason.
All the color began to drain from my vision, to my dismay...
though my mother didn't seem too concerned...
Why, your eyes must be calibrating themselves for your new life with the Monochrome Prince!
How diligent you are!

As more months passed, I lost my appetite and developed a persistent stomachache.
Eventually, my parents decided to keep me on permanent bed rest in the infirmary.
They were getting desperate to cure whatever was ailing me in time for the wedding.
Hello?
knock
knock
I'm Asa, your nurse. I'll be handling your daily regimen from here on.
Ah, thank you.
I heard that you haven't been feeling well for quite some time, Your Highness.
Yes. It's a persistent and mysterious illlness...
but I need to be fully recovered before my wedding later this year.
Hmm...
Hmm...
...!!
Is there a basis for your invasive staring, or shall I scream for the guards?

Huh?! N-no, Your Highness, I apologize! It's just that—
Well, I'm no doctor, but...
I don't think you have a severe, mysterious illness.
...What?
I think you're just in desperate need for some fresh air and sunlight.
Would you be up for going on a stroll with me?
And thus began my series of daily walks through the park with Asa.
So I take it you don't get to go out much, Your Highness?
There's always a never-ending list of duties to complete or topics to study.
I've simply never had time for many leisurely activities inside or outside of our palace.

There's no need to patronize me, Nurse Asa. You help people with real ailments and curses every day.

I'm... honestly very envious of that...

Princesses never have to experience a tough day in their lives...

...so I feel like the very least we can do is not complain about our duties and minor health issues.

I'm not sure about that, Your Highness.

I'm from the Oval Kingdom originally, but I've traveled and worked in the infirmaries of several kingdoms.

But it's seen as a source of shame for their kingdoms, so they're always forced to mask any defects or are hidden away from society entirely.

Or far worse that that...

...I've even heard rumors of a princess born with the curse to occasionally foresee omens of misfortune.

She's held in captivity by her own kingdom, utilized as nothing more than a private tool for their own prosperity and profit, as well as by certain wealthy circles within the black market.

It's people like her who need help and care the most, but I can't reach them.
So I don't blame any princess who complains or takes any advantage they can to help themselves.
I think it should happen a lot more.

...
clench
Ah! But there are wonderful things about the outside world too, like—
Papa Asa! Papa Asa!!

You guys...!
dash~

You have quite a large, diverse horde of offspring.
How could you possibly think I fathered all these children?!

I volunteer at one of the local orphanages during my free time.

And it's been overfilled, so these four buddies have been staying at my house lately.

Papa Asa, are you playing in the park too?

I'm hungry! Make us your apple bread pudding!!

Well, my job right now is to take care of Miss Calpernia, so—

Ow...!

—Your Highness!! Is your stomach hurting again?!

grumble~

...No, I think I'm just hungry too.

After that day, I began spending more time with Asa and his children from the orphanage.

It was there that I first learned how to cook...

Yay! Good job!

You did most of it...

I also learned that the most fun things to do don't actually cost much money...
Nice one!!

...and that I could actually laugh until I cried.

A few months later...
Is this a present? For me?

I-I know it's still a little early for your birthday, but...
I wanted to give you this. Please open it later when you're alone.

Okay. Thank you, Asa!!

Maybe it was the fresh air...
or maybe it was the bread pudding.
Whatever Asa was doing was working, and my world was starting to look vibrant and colorful again.
I was finally feeling better.
But that also meant...
Wow...
You're even lovelier in person, Princess Calpernia.
The Prince of the Monochrome Kingdom...!!
Wh-what brings you to our palace?!
Please, call me Prince Whitney...
It's almost time for you two to get married, dear!
So we figured since you've been feeling better, we'd invite Prince Whitney over so you two can become better acquainted!
That... sounds lovely.

Several hours later...
Finally, a second alone this evening...
Feigning laughter is so much harder once I've experienced the real thing.
rummage
I told Prince Whitney I needed to use the ladies' room...
...but I could really just use a comforting note from Asa right now...
"Dear Calpernia...
It's usually the birthday girl who gets to make a wish, but please forgive me for selfishly making one instead.
I wish for you to call off your betrothal to the Monochrome Prince...
"...and choose me instead...
because I've fallen deeply in love with you."
"I know. It's delusional to even ask a princess to be with a poor man such as myself.
But if there is any chance at all, please accept this necklace. It's my family's heirloom from the Oval Kingdom."

Asa...
All I could think at that moment was, "I should be happy..."
He was the most wonderful and caring man I've ever met. And being around him had changed my life.
But for some reason...
...my stomach pain just doubled.
Why were these the only kinds of opportunities ever afforded to me?
What do you have there?
GASP!

Prince Whitney!!

At that moment, I couldn't help but remember what Asa said...

I don't blame any princess who takes any advantage they can to help themselves.

I-it's a love letter from someone else!

So I'm sorry, Prince Whitney. B-but I can't marry you!!

Tell me— who was that letter from?!

I-it was from the nurse who cared for me...

...Is that so?

What a rotten, deceitful woman you turned out to be.

...Oh.
Well I think we could work around that.
That's kinda hot.
Um... just checking, but...
you do know that men can be nurses too, right?
WHAT?!!
grab
You know what? I'm fine with it.
So let's arrange a little date with you and your lover boy...
where I can give my best regards...

The next evening held the greatest regrets of my life.

Regrets...? Wait, back during the slumber party...

Prez is going to marry a poor man, live in a one-bedroom house with a white picket fence, and have four children.

...Hey! Doesn't that kinda sound like what you—
—Oh my God, I'm so sorry! I don't know what I was thinking...

And when I tried to ask her about her curse...
Um, Prez? What would you do if **you** had your curse removed for 24 hours?
...Nothing.
I can't take back the things I've done.
I can only take my past experiences and try to do something with them that can help others in the present.

What could have possibly happened...?!

So the night after the Monochrome Prince confronted me about Asa...

Calpernia?
swing

I received your message and ran here as soon as my shift at the infirmary was over.
I'm happy you want to see me, especially after the letter I sent you...

I-I'm happy to see you too, Asa...

Y-you're wearing the necklace I gave you...!
Wow, you look absolutely stunning.

Can't say the same about you, though.

So this is my competition?! Unbelievable.
step
step
This is the least sexy nurse I've ever seen.

What...?
Uh, Calpernia, wh-what's going on here...?
Asa quickly realized that the Monochrome Prince had arranged this meeting with ill intentions in mind...
and that I had knowingly lured him here like the rotten, deceitful woman I truly was.
But what could I possibly do to stop it?
My only skill in life was to do exactly what I was told to do...
AH!
Grab
A man who tries to steal a prince's fiancé isn't a man at all, but an **insect**.
PRINCE WHITNEY! PLEASE, STOP!!
And insects deserve to be **squashed**!

Nothing in my life was what I actually wanted.
So then why...
...was I going along with any of it?
ASAAA!!
DASH~
...Whoops.
Oh my God, Calpernia! Wh-why would you...

Because...
You're a father of four children who love you...
and I...
I don't want to marry anyone.
...Once again, you realize those aren't my actual children, right?

Well, it was obviously meant for you, dummy.
It was going to create a very convenient way of disposing of you.
But it looks like I'll just have to do it with my own two hands now.

Calpernia!!
Can you hear me?!
Wait...
a syringe?!
What did you stab her with?!
Slump

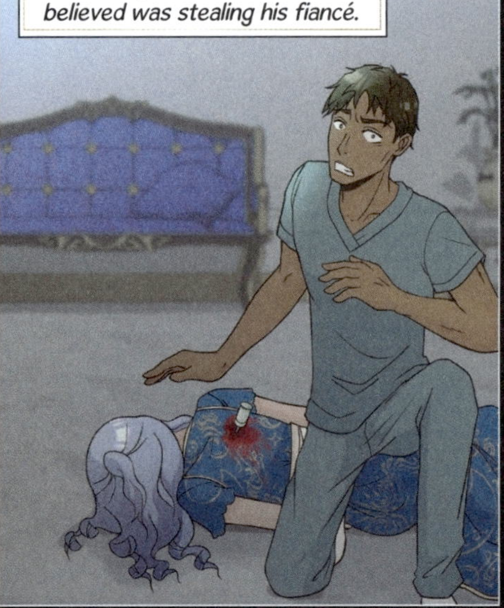
Earlier that day, Prince Whitney had secretly concocted a plan for revenge on the man he believed was stealing his fiancé.

He sent his royal servant to one of the rare curse dealers on the black market.
Fetch me a cursed serum to transform a man into a common house spider.

He would inject him with the curse...
...and crush him under his foot with no trace of his body. It would be the perfect murder.
STOMP!
But unbeknownst to the prince, his servant didn't pick quite the correct transformation curse...
Rabbit, tiger, bird...
Where's spider?
Can I help you find something, ol' man?
Where's spider?
...Oh! Sure.
Lemme grab it for ya.
Why thank you, lad!
WERE-SPIDER

...it wasn't exactly what the prince had in mind.

AAAAAH!!!

The next morning, I woke up on the floor.

I could only vaguely recall brief flashes of the past night.

But when I looked around in a panic, I realized...

Asa...? Asa, where are you...?!

Oh! Whew...So the Monochrome Prince was fine too?
sigh~

Um...
Yeah, no.
I ate him.

You **WHAT**...?!

Not long after I woke up, I felt something lodged in my throat.
blgh..!

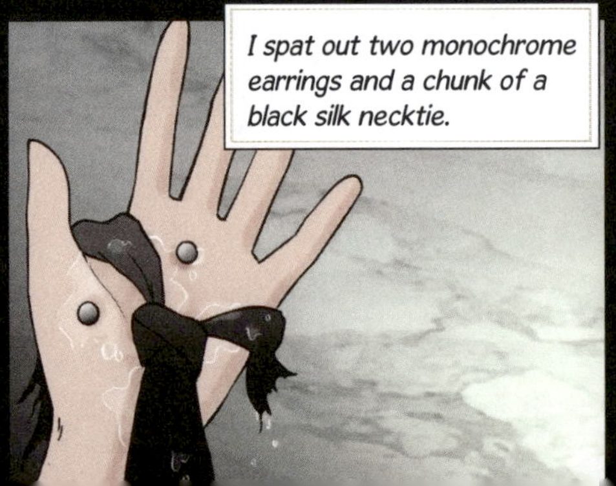
I spat out two monochrome earrings and a chunk of a black silk necktie.

I swallowed him whole, though like much of the rest of the night, I only recall short, vague memories.

So yep.
That's my big regret. I ate an entire man.
Can you still treat me the same, knowing that...?

I-it's no biggie...
Y-yeah...It wasn't in your control...
Why aren't either of you looking me in the eye anymore, then?!

Wait a second... So you turn into a giant were-spider? Like once a month under a full moon?
That can't be true! Two months ago under a full moon, we all played shadow tag and ate s'mores.
And I'm pretty sure it was **your** idea!

Um, well, about that...

The were-spider curse works by latching onto some monthly phase at the time it was activated.
But... instead of a phase of the moon...
it latched onto a different "time of the month" that I was on that night...if you get what I mean.

I-in other words...
I turn into a giant, ravenous, deadly spider once a month during my period.

...Oh.
Gross.

I just told you I ate my ex-fiancé, but **that's** what you're grossed out by...?
...Sorry.

Saffron, how could you NOT have known about Prez's curse up until now?
Why did you think we shut things down every month?

I **tried** to tell him!
But every time I started talking about my period, he'd cover his ears and—
I'm **sorry**!! I wasn't raised around many girls!!
Can we maybe talk about something else, please?!

Um...I would like to hear the rest of your story, actually.
Like what happened to you and Asa?

Oh, right! Well...

Both families soon heard of what unfolded that night.
Because there was so much violence, scandal, and shame on both sides...
it was ultimately decided that the only way to keep peace between both kingdoms was to simply cover everything up and agree to never speak of it again.

But the one condition was that I, the unwed, cursed princess with a murder to my name...
...was to be banished permanently from my kingdom.
But in a moment of compassion, my father made secret arrangements...
for me to live in his abandoned vacation home in the forest of some quaint little kingdom.
It's okay, darling. This is why we have multiple daughters.
...In case one of them commits murder.
And just between you and me, that prince seemed like a butt nugget anyway.
Before I left forever, I met Asa in the park once more to return his family heirloom.
Here. You deserve someone far better than me anyway.
You helped me so much. And in return, I led you on and almost got you killed.

Honestly, the night you wore it...

...I had never seen you be more courageous...
...more honest...
I don't want to marry anyone...
...or more beautiful.

So please, don't regret getting me involved.
And if that necklace helps you to continue living with courage and honesty, then please keep it.

Yeah...I think I'll just be living in shame from now on...
...I've kinda lost everything.

Well... That might be a good thing, Calpernia.
Maybe when you lose everything, it's the perfect opportunity to find out what you truly want to do.

...What I truly want to do...?

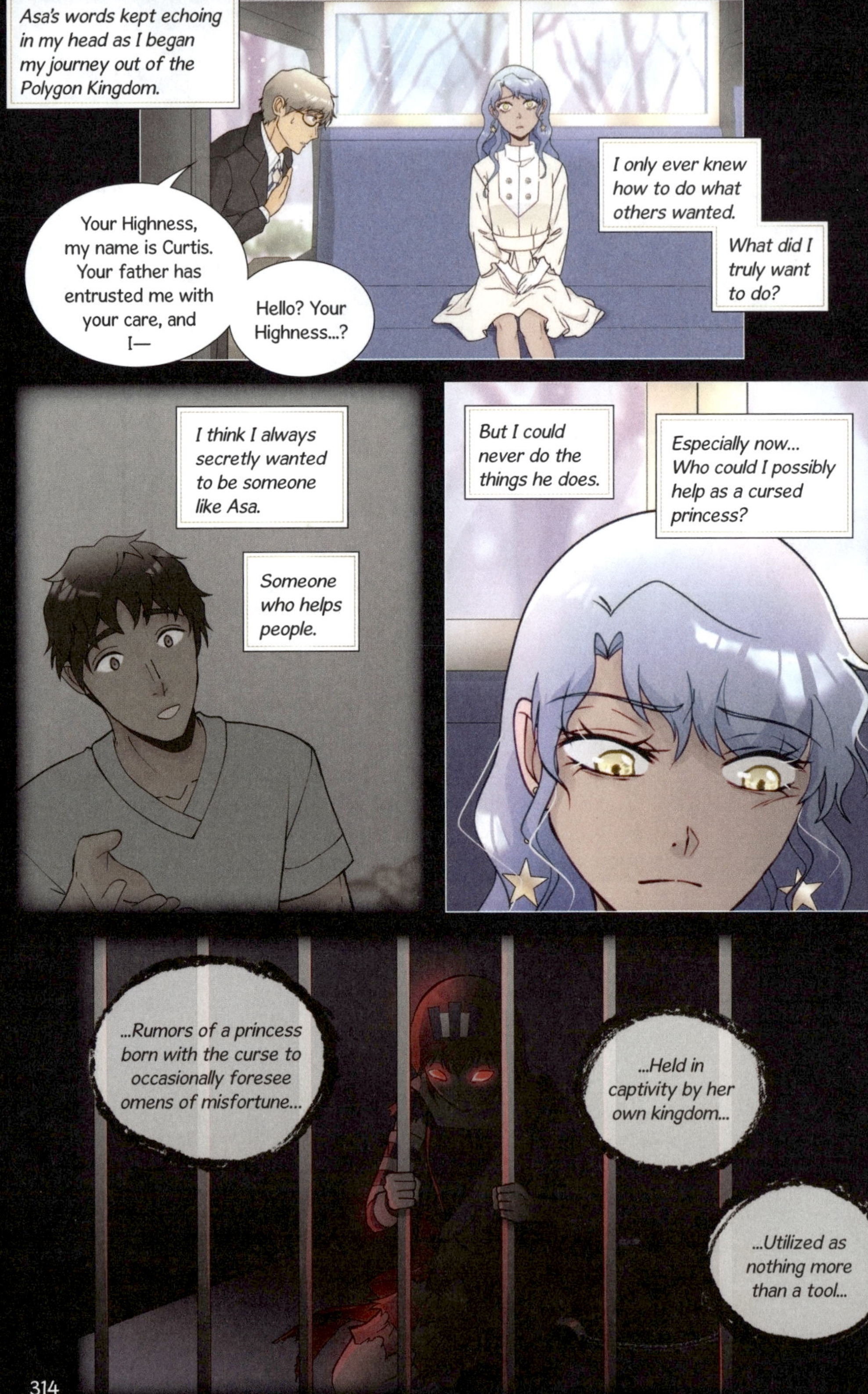
Asa's words kept echoing in my head as I began my journey out of the Polygon Kingdom.
Your Highness, my name is Curtis. Your father has entrusted me with your care, and I—
Hello? Your Highness...?
I only ever knew how to do what others wanted.
What did I truly want to do?
I think I always secretly wanted to be someone like Asa.
Someone who helps people.
But I could never do the things he does.
Especially now... Who could I possibly help as a cursed princess?
...Rumors of a princess born with the curse to occasionally foresee omens of misfortune...
...Held in captivity by her own kingdom...
...Utilized as nothing more than a tool...

It's people like her who need help and care the most, but I can't reach.
For the first time in my life, I began planning my own future...
and became lost in thought for the rest of the trip.
The perfect opportunity, huh...?
step
step
Here we are, Your Highness.
Welcome to...
your new home.

This poor girl has been through so much lately.
I fear her illness will return in full force...
...

Your Highness... Please know that I am here to help you with anything you need at all.
I hope that you aren't feeling too sad about your new arrangements.

...Feeling sad?
There's no time for that, Curtis.

There's a princess that needs to be saved!
But I can't do it unless I can be strong.
Will you help me, Curtis?
Will you help me become strong?!

...

Of course, Your Highness.

For the next few months, all I did was train under Curtis's **unique** tutelage.
cough
cough
There are twenty mattresses in this mansion that will need a good dusting every day.

As much as I was hesitant to trust in his odd methods...
YAAAH!!

...it seemed like butlers really knew how to fight.

Every day, without rest, I trained my body to its limits.

...Well, except for the days I turned into a spider.
knock
knock
Your Highness, I made you a protein shake—

GROWWWL
AAAH!
I-I'll leave it at the end of the hall!!

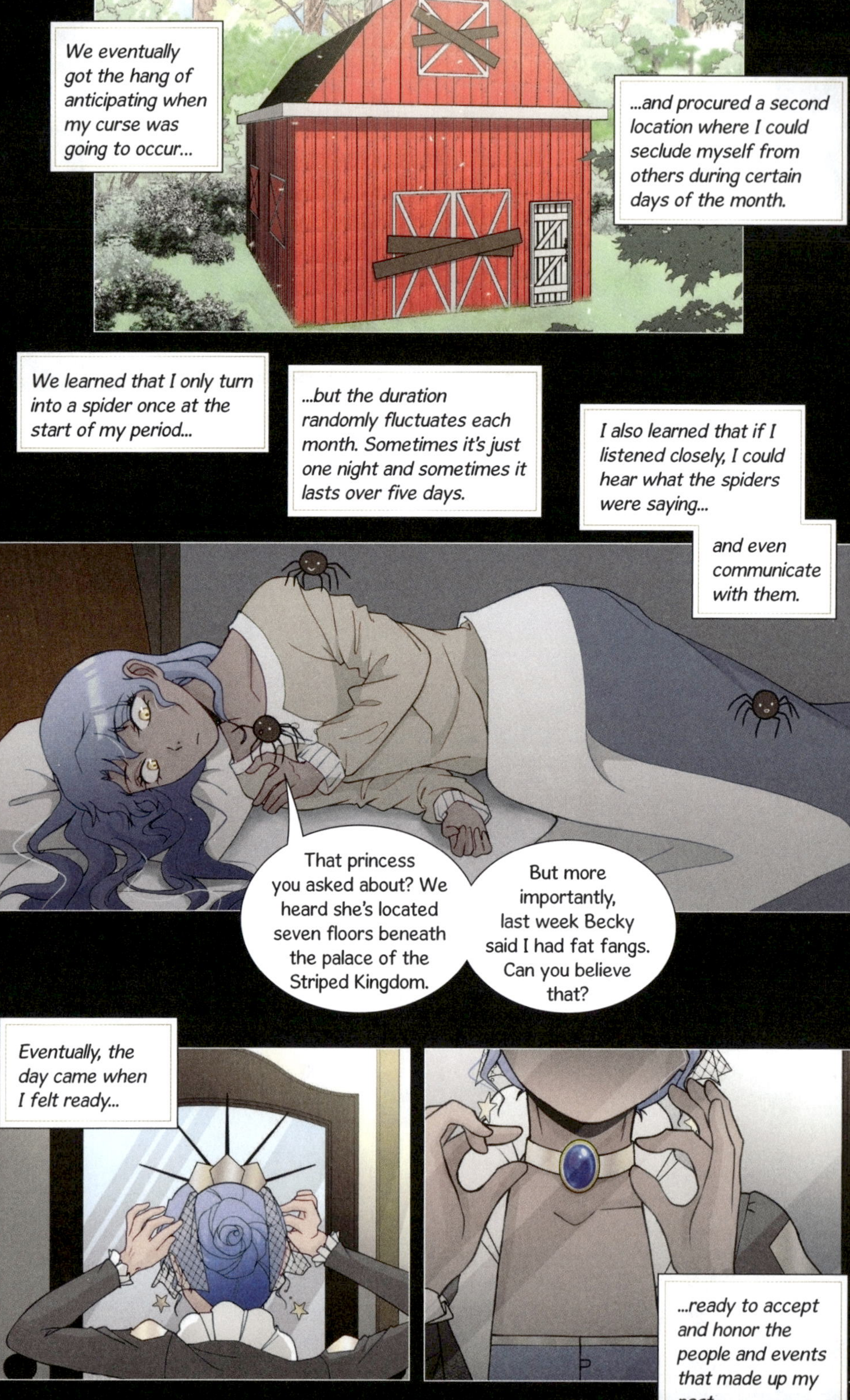
We eventually got the hang of anticipating when my curse was going to occur...
...and procured a second location where I could seclude myself from others during certain days of the month.
We learned that I only turn into a spider once at the start of my period...
...but the duration randomly fluctuates each month. Sometimes it's just one night and sometimes it lasts over five days.
I also learned that if I listened closely, I could hear what the spiders were saying...
and even communicate with them.
That princess you asked about? We heard she's located seven floors beneath the palace of the Striped Kingdom.
But more importantly, last week Becky said I had fat fangs. Can you believe that?
Eventually, the day came when I felt ready...
...ready to accept and honor the people and events that made up my past...

...and ready to begin my mission toward becoming who I wanted to be.
Hold on, Princess. I'm coming for you.
Um, Your Highness... You look very dashing, but...
aren't we going undercover today?
knock knock
AHH dang it, I forgot...!
NOW I was ready for my mission.
scrunch
But as it turns out, things really never go as smoothly as you plan.
Oh my God... What the heck was I thinking?!
pant
I wasn't ready for this at all!!

I lost all my weapons, and I almost died like eight times...
The royal guards are gonna find me soon...
and I still have no idea where this cursed princess is in this giant prison!!

We can help you...
Who's there?!

Yeah, you, the lady with the giant hands.
If you help us out of this cell, we can tell you how to get to the princess.
Giant... hands...?

What?! No way! Why would I ever trust some locked up prisoners?!
What are you in here for, huh? Assault? Murder?!
HEY!! We may be Princels, but we're the kind that don't condone violence!

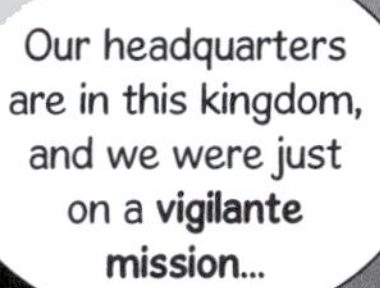

Our headquarters are in this kingdom, and we were just on a **vigilante mission**...
of breaking into art museums and painting over portraits of handsome princes so that they're just **slightly uglier**.
Okay, now make his ears a little wider...
Guys! Someone's coming!!

But we were caught, and they won't believe that we're princes!!
And it turns out that defiling a royal portrait here is punishable by **death**!!
PLEASE! SAVE US!!
The guards are coming to take us to our execution any minute!!

Well, death seems a little extreme...
but I dunno...I kinda got my hands full—
Agh... okay, okay!

step
step
step
All right, boys, it's time to go.

Let's keep this nice and easy—
clink

HYAA!
I'm so sorry!!
CHOP!

CHK

Thanks, Ham Hands.
The princess is behind that door. You should be able to get in with that guard's key ring.
Ham Hands...?
DASH

Thanks to the Princels, I miraculously managed to escape from the Striped Kingdom with the cursed princess in tow.
Hurry, Your Highness!!

I couldn't believe it. I found her, and she agreed to come with me!
sigh~
And we were going to live in our new, peaceful sanctuary for cursed princesses.

Princess!
Princess, you're safe now! You can come out—

HISSSS!!

AAAH!!

M-more members...
I think we just need more members...

And that's how the Cursed Princess Club started!
As a place for princesses to help each other become strong and live without fears or regrets—

And yet it's mostly just a place where we eat junk food and hide from the world.
chomp
chomp

What the heck are you guys eating now...?
I'm sorry, I heard someone mention s'mores earlier...

Hey, Gwen, want a s'more—?
Oh...! She's asleep. I guess it is really late now...

Allow me, ladies.
I'll take her into the house.
Thanks, Curtis!

Hey, Curtis, before you go, I've been meaning to ask you...
Earlier this evening when I was a spider, did you happen to...

...kick me in the face?

GASP
I-I'm so sorry, Your Highness!!
I acted impulsively when Gwen was in danger inside the barn, and—

Thank you, Curtis.

If I had taken another life, I don't know how I could go on.
So thank you for saving both Gwen **and** me.

...Of course, Your Highness.

SHRIEK!!

You have **no idea** how angry I am about what you did to Gwen.

SNAP

AAAAH!!

GASP

lift
Oh...! I'm still at the CPC.
What time is it?!

Whew, it's only five thirty in the morning.

There's still time to sneak home before Papa notices I was out all night...

But also...
step
step

There's time to pick something up on the way home...

Chapter
10

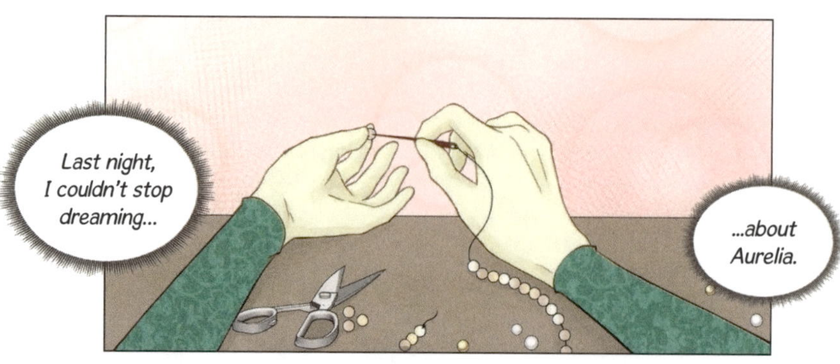
Last night, I couldn't stop dreaming...
...about Aurelia.

The point is that she doesn't belong here.
SHE'S NOT CURSED.
SHE'S JUST UGLY!!!!
It wasn't as if those words weren't hurtful to hear...

But I noticed...
...that it didn't hurt nearly as much as the first time I heard them.

And it's all because...
I could feel their warmth and support around me.
Whereas Aurelia...
She won't get to have that anymore...

dash
It's still really early, so I think I'll make it in time...

I'm getting way too good at sneaking out of the palace.
push
Maria would be so proud if she knew...
I'll just do my usual quick scan to see where the guards are stationed today...

Gasp!
Wh-what's going on out there?

Why are there so many guards out?!

Listen up, everyone!
There was another terrifying growl echoing out of the haunted forest last night!
So we've received strict orders from the higher-ups...
to increase our security around the castle perimeter!

As lieutenant, it's my sworn duty to do everything I can to protect our princesses!
And I won't allow anyone to sneak in or out of this palace...
be it man, beast, or stupid, beefy, hot prince...

No...! That means I won't be able to make it to the club today!
What do I do?!
Morning, Gwennie!
J-Jamie!!
step
step
Whoa, what's wrong, Sis?
Um, I-I can't tell you exactly...
I know I'm only allowed to leave the palace during my scheduled extra-curricular activities...
...but I really, really need to go somewhere right now...
and I can't because all these guards are outside. And—
Say no more, Gwennie.
It's time I did something I should have done long ago.
J-Jamie, wait! It's okay, you've done enough for me lately...!
Don't worry, this is for all of my sisters!

All right, you three head over to the back—
HEAR YE! HEAR YE!!
step
step
As Prince of the Pastel Kingdom...
Is that Jamie's voice?
I demand that my sisters be granted the right...
to leave and enter the palace of their own free will!
And until these demands are met...
...I shall only wear my new protest garments!!
These were sewn with the **finest** materials...
...by tailors who once made clothes for a highly respected emperor!!

What the...?
He's very obviously just naked...
JAMIE, YOU'RE THE FRICKIN' BEST!!
YASSSS, JAMIE!!
...
Guards! Stop standing around...
and clothe my son!!!!
You'd better catch me before I make it into town!!
I heard it's Bottomless Brunch at Little Miss Muffet's Buffet!
dash~
Thank you for the distraction, Jamie!
I'll bake him some cupcakes later...
tip toe

Meanwhile, in the kitchen of the Cursed Princess Club Headquarters...
Hey...Whose dumb idea was it to stay up the rest of the night drinking?

Um, that would be you. You said you wanted to forget as much about last night as possible...
So we all promised to keep you company.
Oh. Right. Welp, I guess it's working.

You need to stop blaming yourself, Prez.
For what happened with Gwen **and** Aurelia.

I don't know about that...
I just got so enraged when I learned that I almost murdered a second person because of her actions.
But I'm not sure if it was rage toward her or toward myself.

I also can't really blame her for her confusion about the club's purpose.
This started out as a club just for princesses with curses.
But I've always wondered if there were people out there who we've never met and don't have curses...
who could be helped by what we do too.

People out there who don't treat themselves with love.

People who are ashamed to share their true selves with others.

I ♥ BLAINE

And people who are struggling to realize what it is that they truly want...

step
step

...And we're one hundred percent sure Gwen's not cursed?
Where are my glasses? I got the munchies...

Saffron! That was settled the day we met her!
Gwen says she's not cursed!!
Okay, okay, I'm sorry!! She just sort of...looks like—

Hey, guys! Speaking of Gwen. Look!!
She left us some souvenirs from that party at the Plaid Palace!
I think these are Plaid truffles!!

What's in this envelope?
Aww, I think it's a commemorative portrait—

WHOA.

Live. Laugh. Laverne.

Guys...Are you thinking what I'm thinking?
OH yeah.
nod nod
Definitely.

Gwen's dad is **super hot**!!
Gwen's sisters are super hot!
That llama's really pretty...

step
step

Aurelia!! Wait!
Jeez, can't these people even let me leave in disgrace quietly?

cough
pant

Wow. You ran over just to rub it in that you won?

No, I... *wheeze*
...came to bring you this...

My favorite necklace...

SNAP
She picked up all of the beads from last night...
and put it back together...?
AAAAH!!

There's so much I want to say to Aurelia...
but I'm not very good at words...
I want to tell her that she's right...
I don't deserve to be in the Cursed Princess Club. And I've leaned on their support for too long.

But I want to stay...
...and do my best to help them just like they've helped me.
And I hope that she can return.

I don't know how to tell her that, so...
all I can do is hope that some of it is passed through this necklace.

...
You know, Gwen...

I feel sorry for that fiancé of yours.

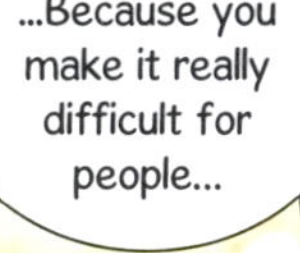
...Because you make it really difficult for people...

once they realize they were wrong about you.
step
step
See ya.

I don't really understand what Aurelia meant...

...but maybe it's another thing I can try to get better at.

I wonder if the coast is still clear for me to sneak back into the palace...

gasp

Oh.

There you are...

To be continued in *Cursed Princess Club* volume 3

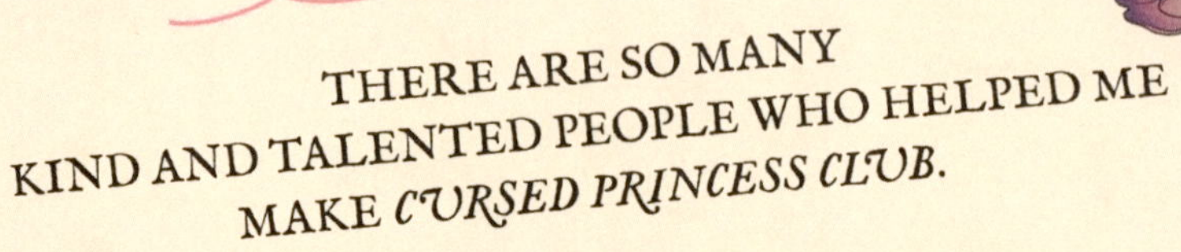

THERE ARE SO MANY KIND AND TALENTED PEOPLE WHO HELPED ME MAKE *CURSED PRINCESS CLUB*.

Thank you...

...to WEBTOON and Eunice Baik for giving me an opportunity I could only dream about. ❤ To Bobbie Chase for all her expertise, guidance, and patience, and for letting me be a part of this amazing experience of making a book. ❤ To Niko, Pat, Josh, Delaney, Emma, Tammy, Rachel, Maeve, Alec, Sera, and everyone on the Wattpad WEBTOON team for helping elevate this story in endless ways. ❤ To my immensely brilliant art assistants Shei, Catburgerhelper, ShiHwi, Kyorin, Meesh, and Alex who shared their talents with me in making this comic, and then didn't run away when I suggested the ridiculous idea that we should do it all over again for the books. ❤ To Taylor Grant for always being a champion for CPC. ❤ To Dayna Broder for consulting me on fencing for this volume, even though I broke all the rules anyhow and it barely resembled fencing by the time I was through with it. ❤ To my partner of twelve years, G, for being my best friend and life support and best maker of breakfasts. ❤ To everyone who's holding this book and to everyone who has ever read and supported *Cursed Princess Club*, I'll truly never be able to say it enough: thank you so, so much.

May we all live, laugh, and Laverne,
LambCat

LambCat is a small, omnivorous,
and easily frightened creature who has burrowed deep
into the Pacific Northwest to draw comics and make music.
They can be lured out by Bill Evans records and
frosted animal crackers.

Read the original on www.WEBTOON.com